Julie

1974

Takes a Stand

by Megan McDonald

★ American Girl®

A Peek into Julie's World

Julie lives in an apartment right above her mother's second-hand shop, Gladrags. If her mom needs her help in the shop, Julie just pops downstairs.

Julie likes to decorate her bedroom with homemade crafts.

Julie loves to play basketball. But no bouncing the ball in the apartment!

Julie's Family and Friends

Mom
Julie's mother,
who runs a store

Dad
Julie's father,
a pilot

Tracy
Julie's sister,
who is 15

April
Julie's cousin,
who is 13

Joy
A girl in Julie's class,
who is deaf

T. J.
A boy at school

Table of Contents

Flying

✿ Chapter 1 ✿

Julie lifted her long calico dress to lace up her shoes. Then she smoothed her apron and tied the strings of her sunbonnet. "How do I look?"

"Like a real pioneer," said Mom, taking straight pins from between her lips. "I have to finish off this hem. Dad'll be here to pick you girls up first thing in the morning."

As Mom pinned up the hem of the pioneer dress, Julie hugged herself with excitement. Tomorrow Dad was taking Tracy and her to the airport. They were flying east to Pittsburgh, where Julie and Tracy would join their Aunt Catherine, Uncle Buddy, and cousins Jimmy and April to celebrate the Fourth of July.

But this was not just any July Fourth celebration, Julie reminded herself. It was 1976, the Bicentennial, and Julie and her sister were going to be part of a very special event. An old-fashioned pioneer-style wagon train, with wagons from all fifty states, was crossing the country in honor of America's two-hundredth birthday. Except unlike in the pioneer days, this wagon train was starting on the West

Coast and heading east, all the way to Pennsylvania. "It's like history in reverse," Dad had put it. In Pittsburgh, Julie and Tracy would join their cousins on a horse-drawn wagon for the last three weeks of the journey.

Julie shivered with anticipation. An airplane . . . and a covered wagon! She would be like Laura Ingalls Wilder, who had crossed the prairie with her family in the Little House books. Julie could hardly wait.

Tracy stopped brushing her hair and held up the green and white cotton dress Mom had made for her. "Did pioneers really wear these long dresses and ugly aprons? I'll die of embarrassment if I have to wear this. I look like Raggedy Ann."

"You can wear blue jeans on the wagon," said Mom. "But take the dress—you may want to wear it when you get to Valley Forge."

"Think of it as dressing up for a giant birthday party for our whole country," Julie said. "Just think, two hundred years ago was the original Fourth of July, with the Declaration of Independence." Julie held up a hairbrush in a dramatic pose. "Give me liberty or give me death!"

"Give me my hairbrush," said Tracy, grabbing the brush and stuffing it into her overflowing suitcase. "Okay, I'll take the dress, but I need a second suitcase. I haven't even packed my pillow yet, or my magazines, or—"

"Why not take your tennis racket, and your hair dryer, and your princess phone?" Julie asked, turning to admire her pioneer outfit in the mirror.

"Ha, ha, Julie Ingalls Wilder," Tracy teased back.

Mom smiled. "I sure am going to miss you girls," she said, handing each of them a gift.

Julie unwrapped her present. Inside was a blank book covered in fabric with orange pop-art daisies. "A journal!" She hugged the book to her. "Thanks, Mom. It's perfect."

"A trip like this is a once-in-a-lifetime event," said Mom. "You'll want to remember everything that happens."

It didn't take long for Julie to finish packing. From all the weekends she'd spent at Dad's house, she'd become an expert packer. She neatly tucked her pioneer dress on top of her jeans, her T-shirts, and her Little House books.

"Please tell me you're not taking all nine of those books in your suitcase," said Tracy.

"Why not? At least my stuff all fits in one suitcase." Julie glanced at Tracy's two bulging suitcases. "Looks like you're taking your whole closet and half the bathroom."

Tracy shrugged. "So? This way I'll be prepared for anything."

❁

That night, a fluttery mixture of excitement and nervousness kept Julie from falling asleep. She opened her new journal to the first page and wrote:

Things I want to do on my trip:

Ride a horse
Learn pioneer stuff like building a fire
Sleep in a tent
Make friends with cousin April

Julie paused and chewed the end of her pencil. There was something else she wanted to add, but she didn't know quite how to put it. Finally she wrote:

Do something special for my country

She read over her list. The last line looked a little funny. After all, the wagon train was something special. Maybe that was enough. But Julie couldn't help hoping that somehow she could do more than just go along for the ride. The wagon train journey would be a once-in-a-lifetime event, as Mom had said. Julie hoped that somehow she could be a special part of it.

❀

"Buckle up," said Julie's father. "We're getting ready for takeoff."

Soon they were high up in the air. Dad took out a map of Pennsylvania and spread it across Julie's tray table. Julie traced her finger along the route Dad had highlighted. It ended at Valley Forge.

"Dad, how come all the wagons are going to Valley Forge?" Julie asked.

"Well, it's a big park, so there'll be enough space for all the wagons, horses, and people," said Dad. "And two hundred years ago, George Washington and his soldiers spent a long, hard winter in Valley Forge during the Revolutionary War. So it's an important place in history."

"Yeah, they were freezing and starving," Tracy chimed in. "We read about it in school. They didn't have enough shoes, or coats, or food, or anything. A lot of soldiers got sick." She shook her head. "I never would have made it, that's for sure."

Dad chuckled. "Even those soldiers barely made it, but in the end, they pulled through—and turned the tide of the war. And because of them, we're here today, and our country is two hundred years old."

Julie thought back to that winter so long ago. It was

difficult imagining the hardships those soldiers had lived through—and all because they had this idea of starting a new country. Would she be willing to go through that, all for an idea that might not even work? And later, settlers crossing the country in horse-drawn wagons to find new homes had known hunger and sickness, too. Julie looked out the airplane window into the vast blue sky. It was strange to think about George Washington and his soldiers, pioneers like Laura Ingalls and her family, and now her own family flying through the air in a jet plane—and how they were all part of the same country. They were all connected.

Wagons, Ho!

✿ Chapter 2 ✿

I t was still dark the next morning when Julie, Tracy, and Dad headed out of the city to meet their cousins at the crack of dawn. They crossed a long bridge, leaving the glittering lights of Pittsburgh behind them.

"Do you think April will like me?" Julie asked. She could barely remember her cousin, whom she hadn't seen since she was five. "I wonder if she likes the Little House books. Do you think she'll have a pioneer dress, too?" Or would April think it was embarrassing, the way Tracy did?

"I think she'll like you much better if you're not such a Chatty Cathy at five o'clock in the morning," Tracy grumbled. Chatty Cathy was a doll that talked and talked when you pulled her string. Julie knew Tracy was teasing her, but she smiled to herself. Tracy would have to get up early *every* morning on the wagon train!

As the sun began to rise, Dad parked the car near a boat dock. A tugboat was pushing two barges toward the dock. Each barge carried rows of pioneer-style wagons with big white canvas covers. In a silent parade, the wagons came to shore. Throngs of people had gathered at the dock and teams of horses stood patiently, waiting to be hitched up.

"Julie! Tracy! Uncle Dan! Over here!" A long-legged girl with brown hair, bangs, and dimples waved her arms. "It's me, April!" Behind her, Julie recognized Aunt Catherine, Uncle Buddy, and her cousin Jimmy. They all hurried over, engulfing Julie, Tracy, and Dad in a sea of hugs.

Dad stepped back and took a good look at his niece and nephew. "April, I can't believe you're already thirteen. And look at those sideburns on Jimmy." Jimmy grinned, blushing pink to the roots of his collar-length, wavy brown hair. He was eighteen.

"Don't you think he looks kind of like Pa from *Little House on the Prairie*?" asked April. "That's my all-time favorite TV show."

"Hey, those are my favorite books!" said Julie.

"She brought the whole set with her." Tracy rolled her eyes.

"That's why I can't wait to ride in a real covered wagon," Julie said. "Sometimes Laura rode the wagon horses to get water. Do you think I can try riding a horse?"

"You've never ridden a horse before?" April said, sounding surprised. "Wait till you meet Jimmy's horse, Hurricane."

Julie looked at Jimmy. "You have your own horse?"

Jimmy nodded proudly.

"April's a good rider, too," said Aunt Catherine. "I'm sure she'd be happy to teach you to ride, Julie."

"I'm off to get my instructions," Jimmy announced. "See you all at camp tonight!"

"Jimmy's one of the outriders," Uncle Buddy told them. "They make sure the cars don't interfere with the horses on the road, things like that."

As Jimmy headed off, he stopped to shake hands with a man dressed in overalls. "Hey, there's Tom Sweeney," said Uncle Buddy. "Tom! Come say hello," he called. "We have two newcomers joining our wagon."

"Mr. Sweeney's our neighbor—he owns the farm next to ours," Aunt Catherine explained. "He's the history buff who got us going on this trip. It's his wagon and horses we're using."

Mr. Sweeney came over and shook hands with Dad, Julie, and Tracy. "So you're the city folks. Pleased to have you join us on the trail," said Mr. Sweeney, flashing a smile from his tanned, leathery face.

"It's my girls who are joining you," Dad said. "I'm just here to see them off."

"In that case, have you signed the rededication pledge yet?" Mr. Sweeney unrolled a long piece of paper. Across the top, in fancy calligraphy, it read "Pledge of Rededication."

Below was a quote from the Declaration of Independence, with columns of blank lines for signatures.

"By signing this pledge, people are saying they still believe in the principles our country was founded on—freedom and equality, just like it says in the Declaration of Independence," said Mr. Sweeney. "We're collecting the signed scrolls as we roll across the country. At Valley Forge we'll present them to the president. He'll sign one, too."

"*The* president?" asked Tracy. "As in President Ford?"

Mr. Sweeney grinned. "That's the one."

Dad gave a low whistle. "You girls may get to see the president," he said.

Mr. Sweeney went on. "At every town we stop in, people bring us signed scrolls to take to Valley Forge. Would you girls like to help me collect them?"

Julie and April nodded. "I know how to collect signatures," said Julie. "I had my own petition for our school basketball team."

"Great. I'll be glad to have more help," said Mr. Sweeney. "Now, go ahead and sign your own names, if you like." He held out the scroll and offered Dad a pen. Dad and Tracy signed their names and passed the scroll to Julie.

The fancy writing at the top made the scroll look very important. Under the title it said:

To commemorate this nation's Bicentennial we hereby
dedicate ourselves anew to the precepts of our Founding
Fathers: We hold these truths to be self-evident, that
all men are created equal . . .

Julie wrote her name on the scroll, using her best
cursive. It gave her a chill to sign her name to the pledge.

At the dock, the wagons were being rolled off the
barges one by one. A short, stocky man wearing a badge
announced, "Alaska!" as the first official state wagon rolled
down the ramp. A hearty cheer rang through the crowd as
each wagon was eased off the barge.

"That's Mr. Wescott, the wagon master," April told
Julie. "Come on, let's go see our wagon." She led Julie over
to her parents, who were harnessing two heavy brown
workhorses.

Uncle Buddy looked up. "Meet Mack and Molly, two of
the finest Belgian draft horses in Pennsylvania."

Julie held out a hand to Molly, who nuzzled
her with a soft snuffle. Suddenly Molly lifted
her head, ears pricked forward, and Julie
heard thundering hoofbeats. Looking up, she
saw Jimmy riding a tall brown and white
horse. Julie backed up as the horse sniffed
noses with Mack and Molly and then

squealed, tossing his head and prancing sideways.

"Easy, boy," said Aunt Catherine, reaching up to stroke Hurricane's head and neck. She winked at Julie. "He knows he's a beauty."

Julie smiled thinly. She'd been counting the days till she could ride a horse, but now, at the thought of getting on such a mountain of a creature, her knees weakened.

"Don't mind him," said Jimmy, motioning to Julie to come closer. "He's just excited. Go ahead, you can pet him."

Nervously, Julie reached up to pet the horse on the neck. Hurricane let out a low nicker, and Julie snatched back her hand.

Jimmy chuckled. "That means he likes you."

Suddenly the wagon master's voice rose above the hubbub. "Wagons, ho!" he called. "Load 'em up and moooooove 'em out!"

"Time to go," called Uncle Buddy, buckling one of Mack's harness straps.

"Have a great time," said Dad, hugging his daughters good-bye.

"I wish you were coming too, Dad," Julie said as she and Tracy hugged him back.

"I know, honey. I can't take the time off. But I'll meet up with you for the Fourth of July." Dad helped Julie and Tracy up into the wagon.

The wagon had new paint and a warm barn smell. It was crammed full of suitcases, sleeping bags, blankets, food, camping gear, a toolbox, and a bucket of horse brushes.

"I can barely stand up in here," said Tracy, touching the inside of the white canvas cover with her hand.

"I think it's cozy," said Julie.

Soon the wagon wheels were creaking and rolling out of the park and onto the dusty road. The girls waved to Dad as he became smaller and smaller, framed by the horseshoe-shaped opening in the canvas at the back of the wagon.

"See you at Valley Forge," Julie called.

❁

Mile after mile, the wagons rolled past farmhouses, barns, and fields of grazing cows. Perched on a cooler, Julie could see the whole wagon train stretched out behind her like beads on a necklace, disappearing around a curve in the road. There was so much to look at—horses with fancy harnesses, colorful flags flapping, men in buckskin outfits and coonskin caps. Bringing up the rear was an old green station wagon with an American flag on its antenna.

Soon Julie noticed that she could feel every rock and rut in the road under the wagon's wooden wheels. "It's so bumpy, I think my bones are being rearranged," she remarked.

April nodded. "You get used to it after a while."

At last it was time to stop for lunch. The wagons pulled off the road into a park outside a small town. Children who had been playing in the park gathered nearby, gazing at the wagon train with wide eyes.

April nudged Julie as they climbed out of the wagon, saying, "I bet those kids wish they were riding with us!" Julie nodded, proud to be part of such an unusual and important happening.

"I'm so hungry, I could eat a horse," said Uncle Buddy as Aunt Catherine passed out sandwiches.

"Don't say that, Dad—Mack and Molly can hear you!" April laughed.

Julie lay back on the picnic blanket, relieved to have a rest from the bumpy wagon. "This is the best tuna sandwich I've ever had," she announced.

Aunt Catherine smiled. "Food always tastes better on the trail."

Mr. Wescott, the wagon master, approached their group and shook hands with Uncle Buddy. "Tom Sweeney tells me you have two new wagoneers," he said.

Uncle Buddy introduced Julie and Tracy. "This is Mr. Wescott, our wagon master. He rides in the official Pennsylvania state wagon and leads the way. He's the boss, so make sure you listen to him!" Mr. Wescott winked at the girls.

"I'll tell them the rules," said April. "Stay together. Safety first, especially when cars are on the road. And no selling wagon-train souvenirs to people along the way."

Mr. Wescott let out a hearty laugh. "Couldn't have said it better myself. We should make you assistant wagon master. Speaking of souvenirs, I've got to go talk to that fellow." He nodded in the direction of the station wagon with the flag. "He's got a carload of knickknacks. Some of these folks are becoming quite a nuisance—looking for any way to make a buck, I guess." Waving good-bye, the wagon master headed off.

"That car's been following the wagon train all day," said Jimmy.

Uncle Buddy nodded. "It's a free country, so Mr. Wescott can't stop that fellow from using the roads. All he can do is ban him from selling souvenirs from the wagon train itself."

Julie munched on an apple. "When do we get to help collect scrolls?" she asked.

"In a few days," said Aunt Catherine. "But right now, you can help me collect paper plates and apple cores."

"Come on, let's go feed the apple cores to Mack and Molly," said April.

❀

When the wagon train finally
made camp that night, Julie was
so tired that she could barely help
April and Tracy pitch the tent they
were going to share. But before she
turned off her flashlight and went to
sleep, she opened her journal and began to write.

June 15

*First day on the wagon train. It seemed like we covered a lot
of ground, but Jimmy says we went only four miles!*

*After lunch, I walked right up to Hurricane and fed him an
apple core. I don't want April to know I'm a little scared of him.
I still want to ride him (I think). Maybe tomorrow.*

*Tonight Uncle Buddy got out his banjo, and pretty soon
we had a fiddle player, two guitars, and a white-haired lady on
dulcimer around our campfire. We sang along to "Oh, Susannah"
and "She'll Be Comin' Round the Mountain" and ended up
laughing more than singing. I felt just like Laura when Pa used to
play his fiddle!*

*Gotta go. April is trying to spy on me and see what I'm
writing. I'll get her back—by tickling her to death when she least
expects it!*

Lightning Kelley

As the days passed, Julie settled into life on a wagon train. Each morning, Aunt Catherine made oatmeal for breakfast. After breakfast, Julie packed up her bedding and helped April and Tracy take down their small tent. While Uncle Buddy harnessed Mack and Molly, the girls helped load the wagon. Then they all climbed aboard, waving good-bye to Jimmy as he rode off to join the outriders, and took their place in the line of wagons moving slowly out onto the road.

The June weather was fine and sunny, with a welcome breeze. Most days, the girls started out riding together in the wagon, playing games and watching the scenery go by and giggling about everything and nothing. Julie had never heard anyone laugh as much as her cousin April! Just hearing April giggle made Julie crack up, even when she had no idea what the joke was. Sometimes they rode up in front on the buckboard seat with April's parents or walked alongside the wagon to stretch their legs. The hours slipped by in a rhythm as steady as Mack's and Molly's hoofbeats.

*Just hearing April giggle made Julie crack up, even
when she had no idea what the joke was.*

At midday the wagon train usually stopped in a
park or field where the horses could graze. While Tracy
helped Aunt Catherine prepare lunch, Julie and April
liked to wander among the wagons, saying hello to the
other people and horses, and each trying to be the first to
spot Jimmy and Hurricane. One day they found Jimmy
hunched over his saddle, fixing a stirrup strap. Hurricane
was tied to a nearby tree.

Jimmy looked up as the girls approached. "April, would
you mind taking Hurricane down to the stream for a
drink? He's cooled off now." Jimmy had warned Julie that
you shouldn't water a horse that was still hot and sweaty
because the horse could get sick.

April nodded. "Sure. Come on, Julie." She untied
Hurricane's rope and started across the field toward the
creek. Suddenly she turned to Julie. "Hey, want to ride
Hurricane? I'll boost you up."

"Really?" Julie's heart began to pound. "But wait. What
about a saddle?"

"You can ride bareback," said
April. "It's super fun. Here, I'll
give you a leg up." She cupped
her hands to make a foothold. Julie
stepped into April's hand and, in one
swift motion, swung her other

leg up and over the horse. "Hold on to his mane," April instructed.

As April led Hurricane across the grassy field, Julie wobbled from side to side. Hurricane's bare back was slippery. She hunkered down low, clinging to the horse's mane.

"Try to relax," April coached. "Sit up straight and get your balance."

Gradually Julie sat up a little taller, gripping the sides of the horse with her thighs. She eased into the rocking motion of the horse, feeling his warmth against her legs, his back muscles rippling with each step.

"Good—that's it. You're getting it," said April.

"I'm really riding!" said Julie.

"You're doing great! Want to try a trot?" April asked.

"Sure, why not," said Julie.

"Here, take the rope." April tossed the end of the lead rope up to her. Julie let go of the mane with one hand and caught it.

"Now kick him with your heels," April called. She broke into a jog. "Let's go, Hurricane."

Julie swung out her feet and gave the horse a kick. Hurricane shot across the field, heading straight for the creek. *Ba-da-rump, ba-da-rump, ba-da-rump.* All Julie could hear was the beating of hooves and the whoosh of air in her ears. "Help!" she called, but April was already far behind.

"*Hangggg onnn!*" April's voice was nearly lost in the thundering of hooves.

Julie clung desperately to Hurricane's side, one leg barely hooked over his back. She clutched at his mane. All she could see was the ground—and Hurricane's pounding hooves. Dust stung her eyes. Her heart thumped against her rib cage. If she fell, surely she'd be trampled.

Just when Julie thought she couldn't hang on another second, Hurricane came to a dead stop at the creek's edge. Julie didn't remember letting go. She didn't remember flying through the air. All she knew was the smack of cold water and the bite of a large rock under her shoulder. The wind was knocked out of her. She took in a ragged breath and scrambled backward on all fours to get away from Hurricane, who was calmly taking a drink.

"Julie, are you okay?" April asked, helping her to her feet. "Oh no, you're sopping wet. You look like a drowned rat!" She began to giggle.

"It's not funny," said Julie. "I almost got trampled. And after I fell, I could hardly even breathe."

April picked up the lead rope. "You'll be okay. Falling is part of learning to ride. You have to fall at least seven times before you're a good rider."

"Well, forget about learning to ride, then," Julie muttered. "I'm not getting back up on that horse."

"Oh, don't be such a baby. Look, I won't let go of the rope this time, and we'll just stay at a walk."

"I'm not a baby," said Julie, but her voice came out all wobbly and her legs felt like spaghetti. The girls headed back across the field in silence.

"Hey, Julie, just think—this is kind of like the time in *Little House on the Prairie* when Nellie fell off Laura's horse," said April.

Julie glowered at her cousin. "For your information," she snapped, "that was just in the TV show. The *real* Laura never took Nellie riding—she took her into the stream so that Nellie would get leeches on her legs."

"Leeches? Eeww!" April began to giggle. But this time it didn't make Julie laugh.

June 20, after lunch
I don't care what April or anybody says. I'm not getting back on that horse—ever.
(June 20, later)
I reread On the Banks of Plum Creek *for seven whole*

miles. Translation: I am not talking to April.

Reading about pioneers is not the same as doing it. Maybe it wasn't so hard for Laura when she sat bareback on one of Pa's plow horses, but Hurricane is no plow horse, that's for sure.

Here's what's really bugging me: April thinks she knows all about horses and riding, but she should not have let go of the rope. I could have been hurt. Then she wouldn't have been laughing!

April and Tracy are taking a magazine quiz: Are you more like a marshmallow or a carrot? What a dumb question.

I miss Ivy and T. J. And Mom and Dad. And my nice private bedroom with no dumb giggling teenagers.

I never would have made it as a pioneer. Why did I even come on this trip?

❁

At camp that night, Julie helped Uncle Buddy start the cook fire. As she crumpled newspaper for kindling, a picture of an old man holding up a flag caught her eye. "Oldest Man in State Raises Old Glory," said the headline.

"Look at this," Julie said to her uncle. "The oldest man in Pennsylvania is a hundred and one years old! His name is John Witherspoon, and he lives in a town called Hershey. It says he hangs his flag out every day."

"Hershey—isn't that where they make Hershey's chocolate bars?" Tracy piped up.

"Yup," said Jimmy, "and we'll be going through Hershey next week. There's a big theme park, and we get to spend a whole day there."

"You'll love Hersheypark," April gushed. "It has roller coasters, and a skyride, and everything!" Tracy looked excited, but Julie didn't say anything. She loved theme parks, too, but she still wasn't talking to April.

After supper, Tracy and April went into the tent to play a game Tracy had brought called Mystery Date. Julie heard gales of laughter coming from the glowing tent. She sat alone on a log, poking a stick into the dying embers.

Aunt Catherine came over and sat down beside her. "You were awfully quiet today. Everything okay, honey?" Julie nodded. "You've had a long day. Don't you think you should get to bed?"

"I'm not sleepy," Julie replied. How could she sleep in the tent with April and Tracy laughing their heads off?

"That was some fall you took today," Aunt Catherine said gently.

Julie could not keep her lip from quivering. Aunt Catherine put an arm around her, and the two sat in the comfort of the quiet dark.

"Have you ever heard the story of Lightning Kelley?" asked her aunt, breaking the silence.

"Who's that?" Julie asked.

"He was your great-great-great-grandfather Elijah Kelley, but everyone called him Lightning."

"Why?" asked Julie. "Was he famous?"

"In his day he was. You've heard of the Pony Express, right? In 1860, that was the fastest way to get mail through the Wild West all the way to California."

"Yeah, we learned about it in school," said Julie, sitting up straighter. "But I never knew that I was related to one of the riders."

"Lightning was only nineteen when he joined up," said Aunt Catherine, "but he could ride a horse like nobody's business. They say he braved robbers, snowstorms, and mountain lions riding for the Pony Express. One time when he was crossing a river, the current was so strong that his horse got swept away right out from under him. He grabbed those saddlebags full of mail, held them high over his head with the river raging all around, and saved the mail. Not a single letter was lost."

"Was his horse okay?" asked Julie.

"Yes, the story goes that he met up with his mustang three miles downriver." Aunt Catherine smiled. "Now, it really is time for bed."

❁

The next morning, Julie slept late. When she emerged from the tent, Tracy was already back from the showers, trying to dry her long hair over the last of the coals from the morning campfire. "How's the shoulder?" she asked.

"Okay, I guess," Julie mumbled, rubbing it. Her shoulder was a little sore, but that wasn't what was bothering her. She took a bite of cold oatmeal.

"Are you still sulking because you fell off that horse?" Tracy asked.

"It's not just that." Julie wanted to tell her sister how let down she felt about the whole trip. She was scared to ride a horse. Even worse, being friends with April felt impossible. But most of all, she was disappointed in herself. She could feel the disappointment making a lump in her throat to go with the lump in her stomach. She pushed the cold oatmeal away.

"You know, Jules, April was just trying to do something nice for you. She knew how much you wanted to ride a horse."

Deep down, Julie knew Tracy was right. But the disappointment wouldn't go away.

❀

For the first few hours of the morning, Julie decided to walk. It felt good to move, and the sun was warm on her face. She hiked alongside the docile workhorses. *If only*

Hurricane had been as calm as Mack and Molly, she thought wistfully.

In the afternoon, the wagon train began a long climb uphill. Their own wagon slowed to a snail's crawl, dropping behind the others. After several hours, Julie peered into the distance. The road dipped and curved around a massive rock. There wasn't another wagon in sight. She couldn't even spot the green station wagon with the flying flag that always followed the wagon train. And they hadn't passed a town all afternoon. There were just rocks, hills, and trees as far as the eye could see, and the constant buzz-saw humming of cicadas. As the shadows grew longer, the hill grew steeper, and Julie could hear Mack and Molly breathing hard as they strained into their collars. Their coats gleamed with sweat.

April poked her head out the front of the wagon. "How much farther do we have to go today?" she asked her parents.

"Mr. Wescott said we have to make it to the top of this mountain by nightfall." Uncle Buddy looked over his shoulder at the setting sun. "I'm guessing it's only a few miles more, if we're lucky."

"But the sun's already going down," said April. "Where's Jimmy? I wish he'd ride back and tell us how much farther we have to go."

Without warning, the wagon lurched hard to the right and jerked to a stop. "Whooaa!" Uncle Buddy called to the horses. He set the brake and jumped down from the leaning wagon.

"Is everybody okay?" Aunt Catherine asked.

"We're okay," said Tracy. "But what happened?"

"Did we hit something?" asked April.

They scrambled down off the wagon. Aunt Catherine shone the flashlight while Uncle Buddy squatted on the

ground to check under the right side of the wagon. He caught his breath as the flashlight played over the front wheel. It was stuck in a pothole and bent at an odd angle.

"Is the wheel broken?" April asked.

"I'm not sure," Uncle Buddy said tightly. He crouched lower, peering underneath the wagon. "The wheel seems all right—it's the axle I'm worried about. We'll have to get the wagon up out of this hole so I can take a better look."

"Maybe we could help push," Tracy suggested.

"You read my mind, Trace. Catherine, you drive," said Uncle Buddy. "The rest of us will push."

On the count of three, Aunt Catherine snapped the reins and called out, "Giddap! Come on, Mack. Come on, Molly. Let's go!"

"Push," Uncle Buddy ordered.

The horses strained, and the wagon rocked and creaked, but it wouldn't budge. Julie's sore shoulder smarted, and her arms ached from pushing so hard.

"Hold on while I take another look at that wheel," said Uncle Buddy.

Night had fallen. The humming cicadas had given way to a chorus of crickets and frogs and the lonely hoot of an owl. *What if we're stranded here all night, and the wagon train leaves without us in the morning?* Julie wondered. She stole a glance at her cousin. April was chewing a fingernail. *That's exactly what I do when I'm worried,* Julie thought as the last of her hurt and anger melted away.

She walked over and nudged her cousin. "This is kind of like in *Little House on the Prairie* when they were trying to cross a rushing river in their covered wagon," she said. "Pa had to jump into the cold water and swim out in front of the horses to pull them across. Remember?"

April nodded. "And Laura thought they were going to drown, but they made it."

"Girls," Aunt Catherine said, handing a box down to Tracy, "we have to empty this wagon."

"Unload *all* our stuff?" April asked.

"If we lighten the load, we just might get the wagon up out of this hole."

Box by box, one suitcase after another, they lowered everything out of the wagon. The luggage, tents, coolers, and gear made a heap by the roadside.

Clip-clop, clip-clop, clip-clop. A horse's hooves echoed over the night sounds.

"Did you hear that?" asked Tracy, shining her flashlight up and down the road. Like a ghost rider, Jimmy appeared in the small circle of light.

"Boy, are we glad to see you," said Tracy. "We need more hands to help push."

Uncle Buddy came over and handed Jimmy the end of a rope. "Maybe Hurricane can help pull us out of this hole. Here, let's run this rope from your saddle to the wagon. April, you lead Hurricane so that Jimmy can help us push."

Jimmy looped the rope in a half hitch around his saddle horn. He dismounted and handed Hurricane's reins to April.

"Okay, let's try it again," said Uncle Buddy after he'd tied the rope to the wagon. "One, two, three, push!"

Hurricane and the workhorses strained forward. Julie, Tracy, Jimmy, and Uncle Buddy leaned against the back of the wagon and heaved. The wagon gave one loud groan and then lurched over the rim of the pothole.

"Hooray!" the girls cheered.

"C'mon," said Tracy. "The sooner we load back up, the

sooner we get to camp. I'm starving."

Aunt Catherine surveyed the pile. "Girls, this is just too much for the horses to haul up this mountain. We're going to have to make some tough choices and leave some of our things behind."

The cousins looked at one another, stunned. "Mom, we can't just—" April began to protest, but Aunt Catherine was already separating some of the pots and pans.

Tracy opened both of her suitcases and began dividing her things. Into the smaller suitcase went her Mystery Date board game, bathrobe, hair dryer, and extra sweatshirt. She picked up her pioneer dress.

"Not your dress!" said Julie. "You'll want to wear it to the big barn dance when we get to Valley Forge."

"No I won't," said Tracy, stuffing it into the suitcase with her other castoffs. "I look like a dork in that thing."

Julie wasn't about to leave *her* dress behind. But then she thought of Mack and Molly sweating and straining to pull the heavy wagon up the mountain. She thought of Laura Ingalls and the time her family moved to Kansas and had to leave even their beds and chairs and tables behind.

Pulling her suitcase from the pile, Julie lifted out her set of Little House books. If the soldiers at Valley Forge could go a whole winter without shoes and coats, she could do without her books. She took one last look at them and then set the books on the leave-behind pile at the side of the road.

April gasped. "Mom, don't make Julie give up her books. I'll leave my board games and my magazines and—"

"It's okay," Julie told her cousin. "I know all the stories by heart."

"But what will you do now when you're mad at me?" April asked, putting her arm around Julie.

June 21

We (finally!) made it to camp. April and I shouted as soon as we saw the wagons. April always says they look like giant loaves of Wonder Bread. She cracks me up!

Tonight the wagons were circled together around the flickering campfire. It felt like coming home.

Making History

✿ Chapter 4 ✿

June 28, morning

This morning we arrived in Harrisburg, the state capital. Crowds of people stood along the streets to watch and cheer as we rolled past the capitol building. I felt so proud.

We stopped at a large post office to pick up a big box of scrolls. There was a line of people still signing them as we arrived. A girl my age handed me a bunch of scrolls. She said her Girl Scout troop had been gathering signatures since Easter.

June 28, after lunch

April keeps bugging me to ride Hurricane again. She says whenever you fall off a horse, you have to get right back on. I got up my nerve to feed him an apple this morning, but no way am I getting on his back again.

✿

By the time the wagon train pulled into Hershey that night, Julie and Tracy had been on the road for two weeks, April's family had been traveling even longer, and everyone was looking forward to a day off.

The next morning after breakfast, April bubbled with

excitement about the theme park. Julie couldn't wait to go on the rides, but something was nagging at her.

"Why do I feel like I know something important about Hershey?" she asked.

"Maybe because it's famous for Hershey bars?" Tracy said drily.

"And Hershey's chocolate kisses—yum!" April added.

"No, it's something else," Julie said, frowning. Then she remembered—the night after she fell off Hurricane, when she'd helped Uncle Buddy make a fire and had found that newspaper story. The oldest man in Pennsylvania lived in Hershey!

"Hey, April, what if we got Mr. Witherspoon to sign one of the scrolls? He's the oldest man in Pennsylvania— a hundred and one years old—and he lives right here in Hershey!"

"Let's go ask Mr. Sweeney," said April. The girls scurried around the wagons, looking for Mr. Sweeney. They found him sitting on the back of his wagon eating a sandwich. He greeted the girls with his usual cheerful smile. Julie asked him about Mr. Witherspoon.

"Oh, yes, I read that newspaper story," said Mr. Sweeney. "Wouldn't it be something to get his signature on one of our scrolls? But girls, I don't see how it's humanly possible. He lives ten miles out of town, and there isn't time to arrange to send somebody out there. Mr. Wescott has given the out-riders the day off." He shrugged good-naturedly and took another bite of his sandwich. "Too bad, though. Michigan Bob would be green with envy!"

"Who's Michigan Bob?" Julie asked.

"An old pal of mine who's collecting scrolls on the Great Lakes route. I hear he's been bragging since Detroit about some World Series pitcher who signed one of his scrolls. He's hoping he'll be chosen to present the scroll for President Ford to sign. The Bicentennial committee hasn't yet decided who gets to do the honors, but that old fellow's signature might put me in the running!" He winked at the girls and gulped a drink from his canteen.

"Oh well, it was a good idea, anyway," said April as they strolled back to their wagon. "Hey, look, there it is—Hersheypark!" In the distance, the highest tracks of a roller coaster arched above the trees. "C'mon, let's hurry. Don't you just love roller coasters?"

Julie did love them, but somehow riding a roller coaster didn't seem as exciting—or as important—as getting Mr. Witherspoon's signature. In the back of her mind, an idea was forming. Getting the signature seemed impossible, but Julie couldn't stop thinking about it.

"April, listen. Mr. Sweeney said it's not *humanly* possible, but what about a horse?"

"Julie, what are you talking about?" April asked without breaking her stride.

"What if . . ." Julie said slowly, turning to face April. "If we ride Hurricane out to where Mr. Witherspoon lives, maybe we could get his signature."

April stopped in her tracks. "What about Hersheypark?"

"I guess we'd miss it," Julie admitted. "But you can go another time, and we have theme parks in California, too. This is our chance to do something big—but I can't do it by myself. Do you think Jimmy would let us borrow Hurricane? Would your parents let us go?"

April considered. "Well, I don't see why not. I can handle Hurricane like he's Lassie. I could ride in front, and you could ride double behind me, and we'd be together the whole time. But do you really want to? I thought you were afraid to get back on him."

Julie gave her cousin a weak smile. Her stomach did a somersault just thinking about her last ride and how close she had come to being trampled. Could she really muster the courage to climb back on that horse? What if Hurricane got spooked by a snake? Julie's legs turned to liquid, but she didn't let on—she didn't want April to know how scared she was. Lightning Kelley hadn't let a raging river stop him from delivering the mail. And weren't she and April both related to him?

"C'mon," Julie urged, tugging on her cousin's sleeve. "Let's go—before I lose my nerve."

❁

While Julie studied a map, April saddled up and mounted Hurricane. "Just put your foot in the stirrup and grab the saddle horn. It's easy." Julie swung up onto Hurricane's rump behind the saddle and held tight to April's waist.

One nudge from April and they were off. Hurricane started out at a walk. Julie tried to relax and settle in to the rhythm.

"You okay back there?" asked April.

"I think so," Julie said nervously, trying to steady her voice. "It's kind of slippery."

"We'll take it easy, don't worry."

As they rode along, Julie felt more confident and began to enjoy the ride. But her spirits dropped when they reached the first intersection and she checked the map. "We've been riding at least half an hour, and we've only gone two miles. We have eight more miles to go. We'll never make it!"

April hesitated. "Do you want to turn back?"

"No, but . . . what can we do?" Julie's stomach tightened. She knew the answer.

April urged Hurricane across the intersection and

onto the grassy shoulder beside the road. "Let's try a nice smooth canter. You can do it. Ready?"

"Okay," said Julie in a small, shaky voice.

As soon as Hurricane took off, Julie started bouncing and sliding. "Stop!" she shouted. "I can't hold on. I'm slipping off!"

"Whoa," said April, pulling on the reins. When Hurricane came to a stop, Julie clung to April, her heart pounding.

"I have an idea," said April. "You should ride in front so that you can hold on to the saddle horn and put your feet in the stirrups. That'll make it easier for you."

"But I don't know how to steer or work the reins."

"I'll show you," said April. "It's easy."

"Stop saying it's easy!" said Julie. "It's not easy for me."

"Sorry," April said. She dismounted and helped Julie slide forward into the saddle. Then she climbed back on behind Julie and showed her how to hold the reins and guide the horse.

"When you're ready to canter, lean forward a little and squeeze his sides with your heels, gently."

Swallowing her fear, Julie did as April had instructed. Hurricane sprang forward, but since Julie was already leaning forward, she kept her balance.

"Good!" April exclaimed. "That's it!"

"It feels . . . almost like a rocking horse, once you get used to it," said Julie. She was still gripping the horn tightly, but she no longer felt as if she were going to fall. "I think I'm getting the hang of it."

"You're doing great! I knew you could do it. You're a natural."

"I'm riding," said Julie. "I'm riding Hurricane!"

❁

As the girls dismounted, a green station wagon flying an American flag pulled away from the curb in front of Mr. Witherspoon's house.

"Hey, that was the souvenir guy," April said. "I wonder what he's doing here."

Despite the warm summer day, Mr. Witherspoon sat on a front porch seat with a blanket over his lap. His pale blue eyes smiled at Julie from a deeply lined face. "Is the Pony Express delivering my mail today?" he asked, chuckling at his own joke.

Julie pulled Hurricane to a halt next to the man's porch. "I'm Julie, and this is my cousin April. We're from the Bicentennial wagon train. But our great-great-great-grand-father really *did* ride for the Pony Express. His name was Elijah Kelley, but everyone called him Lightning Kelley."

Mr. Witherspoon squinted at them. "Lightning Kelley, eh?"

"We brought a scroll for you to sign," said April, taking it out of the saddlebag.

"It's a special scroll for the Bicentennial," Julie explained, suddenly worried. What if he didn't want to sign it? "If you sign the scroll, it means that you dedicate yourself to the ideas in the Declaration of Independence." There, that sounded impressive.

Mr. Witherspoon frowned. "You're not planning to sell this now, are you? 'Cause the fella who was just here wanted to sell my autograph for money. Even offered *me* money for it. Imagine that." The old man shook his head. "Guess he doesn't know my family's history isn't for sale."

"We'd never sell it," said Julie. "The scroll will be in a museum at Valley Forge." She offered him the clipboard with the scroll.

Mr. Witherspoon reached out a shaky hand and took it. He peered at the heading. Then he looked back up at Julie and April. "You girls know about the Declaration of Independence?" Julie and April nodded.

"Well here's something I bet you didn't know," he continued. "*My* great-great-great-great-grandfather didn't ride for the Pony Express—but he *did* sign the Declaration of Independence."

Julie looked at April and then back at Mr. Witherspoon, her eyes round with amazement. "For real?"

Mr. Witherspoon nodded, his blue eyes crinkling into a smile. "Say, how would you girls like to see a rare copy of the Declaration that's been in my family for two hundred years?"

"We'd love to," Julie breathed.

With effort, Mr. Witherspoon got up from his porch swing. He went inside and returned carrying a slender leather tube. "My hands don't work so well anymore," he said, handing the tube to Julie.

Carefully, Julie and April opened it and slid out a delicate, tea-colored parchment. As they slowly unrolled it, Julie's eyes fell on the sacred words: *We hold these truths to be self-evident, that all men are created equal . . .*

"And there's John Hancock," said April, pointing at the first signature, with its swirling, looping flourish.

The old man pointed a crooked finger at his ancestor's name in the large cluster of signatures at the bottom.

Julie leaned in closer. It was a little hard to read, but she could make it out—*John Witherspoon*. "Wow, he was really there in 1776. Just think—that means he knew Benjamin Franklin and Thomas Jefferson!" Julie looked up, her eyes shining. "You sure are lucky to have this."

"It was lost for many years," said Mr. Witherspoon. "Then one day my mother was getting an old painting framed, and there it was, hidden behind the picture."

"Thank you for showing us," said April, carefully helping Julie roll the parchment back up and slide it into the tube.

"Now, where's that scroll of yours?" the old man asked. "Time for me to sign *my* John Hancock. Or should I say my John Witherspoon? All I need is my quill pen." He reached into his pocket.

"You have a quill pen?" Julie asked, wide-eyed.

His eyes twinkling, Mr. Witherspoon took out an ordinary ballpoint pen, working himself into another fit

of silent laughter. He started to write, but nothing came out of the pen.

"Fiddlesticks!" he said, flipping the paper over and scribbling on the back until the ink started flowing.

"Hey, that scribble looks kind of like the loops under John Hancock's name," Julie remarked to April.

Mr. Witherspoon turned the rededication scroll back over and signed his name on the first line.

John Witherspoon

Julie gazed at his signature on the scroll and then at the tube that held the copy of the Declaration. She felt as if somehow a line had been drawn—a line from the long-ago, dusty past that connected her, today, in 1976, with the birth of the nation two hundred years ago.

June 29 (already?!)

Tracy told me I was crazy to miss Hersheypark. She said it has the best roller coaster ever and lots of FREE chocolate, too! But riding Hurricane was way more exciting than any roller coaster. Coming home, we rode as fast as lightning! (Get it?) And when April and I handed that scroll to Mr. Sweeney and told him how Mr. Witherspoon's great-great-great-great-grandfather had been one of the signers of the Declaration, he could hardly believe it. "Wait till Michigan Bob hears about this!" he said. "That'll put a stop to his bragging."

I think this was one of the best days of my life.

Valley Forge

✿ Chapter 5 ✿

 uly 3, morning

We made it to Valley Forge! There's a tiny town, but most of Valley Forge is a big grassy park with rows and rows of cannons. Huge crowds are here for the Bicentennial. Just think of all the journeys people have taken to get here. Today there's a parade of all the wagons, and tonight is the barn dance. And then tomorrow is July 4, and the president will be here! I hope Dad makes it in time to see him. I can't wait to see Dad, but I'm a little sad, too, because it's the end of our trip.

That evening, after a potluck supper with several other families from their wagon train, the three girls huddled inside the wagon getting ready for the barn dance.

Julie squirmed into her pioneer dress. "Gosh, pioneers sure had to do a lot of buttons," she remarked.

"That's because nobody had invented the zipper yet," Tracy said, zipping up her jeans.

"Tracy, aren't you going to the dance?" April asked.

"Yeah—I'm already dressed," Tracy said, coming over to help. She fastened the top buttons on Julie's dress and

tied a big bow in the sash of April's apron.
"You two look so pretty," she added a bit
wistfully.

"Too bad you left your pioneer dress
behind," said Julie.

"I know," Tracy admitted.
"Everybody'll be in costume tonight.
I'm going to stick out like a sore thumb."

"Knock, knock," called Jimmy from
outside the wagon.

"No boys allowed," said April as Tracy opened the
back flap.

Jimmy looked up at Tracy, holding one hand behind
his back and grinning. He was wearing a fringed buckskin
jacket. His boots were shined and his hair was combed.
Julie thought he looked very handsome.

"Somebody's not going to be filling up her dance card
tonight," he said to Tracy, pointing at her blue jeans.

"Are *you* going to give me grief, too?" Tracy groaned,
but Julie could tell she was kidding.

Jimmy gave her a taunting look. "What would you give
to be able to wear that dress you left behind to the barn
dance tonight?"

"Oh, let me think," said Tracy. "How 'bout a million
dollars?"

"Then you owe me a million dollars," said Jimmy, calling her bluff. He held out a small bundle of cloth tied with twine. "Pay up!"

"My pioneer dress! I don't get it . . . How did you . . . ?" Tracy sputtered, but Julie could tell she was pleased.

"I rescued it that night you guys got stuck on the mountain," Jimmy told her.

"I can't believe it! Where have you been hiding it all this time—Hurricane's saddlebags?"

"Nope, my mom hid it."

"Aunt Catherine, you were in on this, too?" Tracy called.

"Guilty as charged," Aunt Catherine called back. "Now hurry and get dressed. We don't want to be late!"

❀

"That was *so* much fun!" Julie gasped as she and April collapsed on a bale of straw. They had just learned how to square dance. It was a hot night, and the girls had worked up a sweat swinging each other to the lively fiddle music.

"I know—let's cool off by ducking for apples again!" said April. But before they could head to the game area, Aunt Catherine cornered them.

"Time to go, buffalo gals. We've got another big day tomorrow."

"Boy, could I ever use a shower," Tracy said as the cousins walked back to their campsite. "Good thing I don't have to wear this dress again!" She twirled around, making her skirt bell out, and then linked elbows with April and spun her around. Uncle Buddy plucked a few notes on his banjo, while Julie clapped in rhythm, calling, "Swing your partner round and round!"

Suddenly, out of nowhere, Mr. Sweeney came rushing up behind them. "Julie, April—the scroll," he gasped. "It's gone."

July 3, I mean 4

We searched until after midnight, and we still can't find the scroll with Mr. Witherspoon's signature. At first, I was sure it had to be somewhere in Mr. Sweeney's wagon. But it's not, and Mr. Sweeney is convinced it was stolen!

Tracy tried to cheer me up by reminding me that there are still more than twenty million signatures to present to the president. That's a lot of signatures. But are any of them from somebody whose ancestor signed the Declaration of Independence?

❀

The next morning, the whole campground crackled with excitement. Maybe, thought Julie, they'd found the missing scroll while she was sleeping. She hurried over to the fire for breakfast.

"We've searched everywhere," Mr. Sweeney was telling her aunt and uncle. "I have a suspicion, though. That Clark

Higgins, the one who's been selling souvenirs out of his
station wagon—we heard he was after that signature."

April spoke up. "Julie and I saw him that day at Mr.
Witherspoon's!"

"It's wrong to sell Mr. Witherspoon's signature for
money," said Julie. "I promised him it wouldn't be sold.
Can't we make the souvenir guy give it back?"

Mr. Sweeney shook his head. "We would if we could
find him. But Mr. Wescott ran him off again yesterday for
selling without a permit."

After breakfast, Julie and April braided ribbons and

 wildflowers into Hurricane's mane so that
he would look his best for the presenta-
tion of the scrolls to President Ford. The
color guard started the ceremony with a
flag raising and the Pledge of Allegiance.

Everyone sang the national anthem, and then
the governor of Pennsylvania took the podium to read the
Declaration of Independence.

"I can't see," said Julie, standing on tiptoe and craning
her neck.

"Here, sit on Hurricane," said Jimmy. He dismounted
and handed her the reins.

"You mean it?" Julie put one foot in the stirrup, heaved
herself up, and settled into the saddle. It was hard to believe

that only a week ago, she'd
been afraid of Hurricane.

"Make way," said April,
climbing up to sit behind
Julie. "Wow, what a view!"

Hundreds of covered
wagons looked like ships
in an ocean of people. The
fifty official state wagons

were fanned out in formation. Julie scanned the colorful
crowds. People of all ages were wearing everything from
tie-dyed sundresses to cowboy chaps to Revolutionary War
uniforms. Flags flapped in the breeze.

Wait a minute, thought Julie, spotting a familiar-looking
flag—familiar because it was attached to the antenna of a
green station wagon. "I'll be right back."

Before April could ask questions, Julie slipped down
off Hurricane and began weaving her way through the
crowds, dodging horses, strollers, kids, dogs, and Frisbees.
At last she reached the station wagon, half hidden in a
grove of trees.

"Hey!" Julie waved her arms. "Aren't you Mr. Higgins?"

A skinny man standing by the car gave her a friendly
smile. "That's me. I got hats, flags, T-shirts, cuff links, you
name it. I'm your official Bicentennial souvenir shop."

"No you're not," said Julie. "You're not even allowed to be here. I'm reporting you to the wagon master."

"Now hold on just a Ben Franklin minute!" said Mr. Higgins. "What'd I do?"

"Where is it?" Julie demanded. "The scroll with John Witherspoon's signature—the one you stole."

Mr. Higgins's head snapped back and his eyes opened wide. Julie had to admit he looked genuinely surprised. "For your information, missy, I got a seller's permit to be here today." He pulled an official-looking paper with a Bicentennial seal from his pocket. "Go ahead—search my car if you like. I got nothing to hide."

Julie poked her head into the back of the station wagon, but all she could see were boxes and trays of cheap souvenirs. "Well," she stammered, "then how come you're hiding under these trees?"

"A little thing called shade," said Mr. Higgins, pointing to the leafy branches overhead. "It's gonna be a scorcher today."

Julie didn't want to believe him, but she knew she couldn't prove he had stolen the scroll. She didn't feel that she had the right to search his car. Besides, if he had stolen the scroll because it was valuable, he probably had it safely stashed in a hotel room somewhere.

The president was going to arrive at any moment, and

Julie didn't want to miss seeing him. She broke into a run, trying to dodge through the line of official state wagons, but a crowd of people blocked her path. In front of them, newspaper photographers were taking pictures of a man standing at the front of one of the wagons.

"Michigan Bob, what are you going to say to the president?" a reporter called.

Julie paused. "What's going on?" she asked a young woman standing nearby.

"Didn't you hear? Michigan Bob is going to present the scrolls to the president. He has a scroll with a famous signature—"

"Oh, right, a baseball pitcher," said Julie with a nod, remembering what Mr. Sweeney had told her.

"No, this one's from some guy whose ancestor signed the Declaration of Independence," said the woman. "At least, that's what I heard."

Julie drew in a sharp breath. True, there could be many descendants of the original signers, but it was such a coincidence . . . *Something's funny about this,* she thought, frowning. She stepped away from the crowd to get a better look at the wagon. On the side of the wagon, MICHIGAN was painted in big blue letters above a picture of the Great Lakes.

There was no time to waste. Julie darted to the far end of the wagon and quickly climbed into the back.

Desperately she looked around. She knew she was trespassing, but what if the missing scroll was here? It was a slim chance, just a hunch, but she had to take it. Her heart thumped wildly.

She spotted a makeshift desk covered with a jumble of papers. There they were—a whole stack of papers, each full of signatures! *There must be hundreds here*, she thought. *How will I ever find it?* She picked up a pile of pledges and began leafing through them.

"Hey—you there! What do you think you're doing?"

Startled, Julie dropped the papers. "I'm sorry, I—" She bent down to gather up the mess.

"Don't touch those. Just get out." Michigan Bob had come in from the front of the wagon and was making his way toward her.

Julie stood frozen, her eyes riveted on a blank page. It was the back of a pledge sheet, blank except for a small squiggle of hand-drawn loops—loops like the ones under the name *John Hancock* . . .

Julie snatched up the page and flipped it over. There, on the first line, was the signature she was searching for: *John Witherspoon*.

"Hey, gimme that," said Michigan Bob, lunging for her. But Julie was already rolling up the scroll and scrambling out of the wagon.

"Come back here, you!" he shouted as Julie dashed past the crowd and zigzagged across the grassy field around people and dogs, wagons and folding chairs, heading for the Pennsylvania wagon train.

Clutching the scroll, she ran like the wind. *Like lightning*, she couldn't help thinking. *Lightning Kelley.*

Julie was breathless by the time she reached Mr. Sweeney's wagon. Holding her ribs to ease the stabbing pain in her side, she waved the scroll at him, blurting out the whole story.

"You mean to tell me that Michigan Bob stole it right out from under my nose just so he could have his fifteen minutes of fame?" said Mr. Sweeney. "Well, I'll be a star-spangled banana! And to think I considered him a friend."

Word spread like wildfire through the Pennsylvania wagon train that the missing scroll had been found. Cheering and clapping erupted as more and more people heard the good news.

Julie's relatives crowded around, hugging her and patting her on the back. Suddenly Julie felt herself wrapped in a strong pair of arms and swung into the air. "How's my girl? I hear you're a hero!"

"Dad!" Julie squealed. "You made it! I missed you so much."

Dad's long hug told her he'd missed her, too.

"And I thought you just wanted to see the crowd better," said April, starting to giggle. "I didn't know you were going to go all Nancy Drew on us!" Everybody laughed.

The wagon master came over to shake hands with Julie. "I never would have figured it out," said Mr. Wescott. "But I'm awfully glad you did."

"Will Mr. Sweeney get to present the scroll for the president to sign?" Julie asked.

"It's all taken care of," said the wagon master.

"Time out—slight change of plans," Mr. Sweeney announced. "It was Julie who saved the day." He turned to Julie, handing her the scroll. "I think it's only right that you do the honors—present the scroll for President Ford to sign, and shake his hand."

Julie turned a glowing face to Dad. "Did you hear that? I'm going to shake hands with the president!"

Detention

❀ Chapter 6 ❀

ulie's excitement over meeting the president of the United States lasted the rest of the summer and on into her first few days of fifth grade, as she retold the story of the wagon journey to Mom, Ivy, T. J., and her friends at Jack London Elementary. But once school was in full swing, summer's glow quickly faded. One day in September, as she sat in class listening to the teacher talk about the adventures of Lewis and Clark, Julie thought back wistfully to her own summer adventures. She missed that wonderful feeling she'd had at the end of the wagon trip: knowing that she had done something that mattered, something that made a difference.

Maybe it was because her new fifth-grade teacher, Mrs. Duncan, was super-strict. Even her hair was strict—starched and stiff as a ruler. Mrs. Duncan had warned the class against passing notes. So when a note landed on Julie's desk in the middle of social studies, she was intrigued, but cautious. When Mrs. Duncan had her back turned as she wrote on the chalkboard, Julie snatched the note and hid it in her desk.

As Mrs. Duncan talked about Lewis and Clark's trip through grizzly bear country and the Rocky Mountains, Julie snuck a peek at the note. It was from Joy Jenner, a new girl who sat across the aisle from her. When Mrs. Duncan had seated the class alphabetically by first name, Julie and Joy ended up next to each other.

A year ago, in fourth grade, Julie had been new at Jack London Elementary, so she knew just how Joy felt. She was determined to help make Joy feel comfortable.

Julie glanced over at Joy. Joy leaned forward, her dark eyes intent on the teacher's face. Because Joy was deaf, she was trying to read Mrs. Duncan's lips, but she sometimes had difficulty understanding certain words. Julie knew Joy didn't like to ask questions in class, because other kids often snickered at the funny-sounding way she talked.

Quietly, Julie opened the note. It said: *"A sack of wheat saved them?"*

Julie covered her mouth to stifle a giggle. She crossed out "sack of wheat" and wrote, *"Sac-a-ja-we-a, Lewis and Clark's Shoshone Indian guide."*

Julie tossed the note back to Joy just as Mrs. Duncan turned.

"Julie Albright, what have I said about passing notes?" the teacher asked in a sharp voice.

"Not to?" Julie said meekly.

"That's right. You and Miss Jenner have earned yourselves another demerit."

"But Mrs. Duncan, it's not what you think. Joy didn't
understand—"

"No excuses." Mrs. Duncan pointed to the metal waste-
basket. All eyes were on Julie as she trudged to the front of
the room.

"Mrs. Duncan? The note's about our lesson," Julie said.
"Honest. Joy was having some trouble reading your lips."

Joy stood and pointed to herself. In her halting, too-loud
tone, she stammered, "It was my fault. Not Julie's. I passed
the note."

"That's enough, both of you," Mrs. Duncan snapped.
"I will not take up any more class time with this nonsense.
This isn't the first time I've had to speak to you about
this. You will both report to detention after school. Three
o'clock sharp."

Joy looked as if she'd been stung.

"But we only have two demerits," Julie protested.

"Unless you want a whole *week* of detention, you will sit
down immediately. Both of you." Mrs. Duncan set her lips
in a thin, straight line.

Joy slumped down into her chair. Julie's face flushed
red, and she fumed all the way back to her seat. Snickers
spread through the class.

"Any of you are welcome to join them in detention,"
Mrs. Duncan added sharply. "Now take out your silent
reading. I want fifteen minutes of quiet."

Fifth grade was no fair.

*I will not pass notes in class. I will not pass notes in class.
I will not pass notes in class.*

Julie could not imagine writing the same sentence over
and over one hundred times. Her hand hurt just thinking
about it. Then she had to write *I will not talk back to the
teacher* one hundred times. That sentence was even longer!

Julie and Joy were the only girls at the detention table,
along with several boys, including a sixth-grader everybody
called Stinger. Stinger had longish hair that fell over his
eyes. Julie had heard the stories about him. He was always
picking fights on the playground and stealing kids' lunch
money or tossing their bag lunches into the toilet in the

boys' bathroom. Stinger got up
and ambled over to Julie and Joy.

"Mr. Stenger, back to your
seat," said Mr. Arnold, the vice
principal. "We still have half an
hour to go." Mr. Arnold's brown
mustache bristled like a fuzzy
caterpillar.

Julie heaved a sigh and returned to her paper. She was missing shooting hoops with T. J. for this? What a waste.

Finishing her first one hundred sentences, Julie started on the next. Joy looked up and caught her eye. Julie pointed to her paper and then twirled her finger near her temple. She wondered if the sign for "cuckoo" was the same in sign language.

Joy grinned and giggled, copying Julie's "cuckoo" motion.

"Mr. Arnold, they're talking," Stinger said.

"I didn't hear anything," said Mr. Arnold, looking up over his reading glasses.

"That's 'cause they're talking with their hands. I swear."

Mr. Arnold came over to the detention table. "Mr. Stenger, it looks to me like the girls are well ahead of you. Do you need to come up and sit next to me?"

"No, sir," said Stinger.

Julie turned back to her paper. One hour of detention felt like a week. She glanced at a poster near the window. It had a photo of a kitten clinging to a thin branch with the words *Hang in there, baby!*

Only seventy-four more lines to go.

❀

The minute detention let out, Julie was bursting to talk. Joy had to ask Julie to slow down.

"Sorry," said Julie, turning to look directly at Joy so that Joy could read her lips. "It's just that detention is such a waste of time!"

"I know," Joy said. "I don't see what we learned from writing the same sentence for an hour."

"We learned about writer's cramp," said Julie. Joy laughed and made a gesture as if her hand were falling off. Julie laughed, too.

A stern voice behind them said, "Detention is no laughing matter." Julie spun around and there stood Stinger, elbowing his buddies. "Gotcha. I got you so good."

Joy motioned to Julie, pointing down the street. *Let's get out of here.*

"See you tomorrow," said Stinger. "At Detention Club."

"We're not going to be in detention again tomorrow," said Julie.

"Wanna bet? Duncan Donut passes out detentions like sprinkles on doughnuts. She gave me forty-three detentions last year. I hold the school record," he said proudly. "Till you girls came along."

"What was that about?" Joy asked Julie as they hurried down the sidewalk.

"He thinks we're his new detention buddies," said Julie, turning to face her friend. "But I hope we never have to go back there again. Ever."

Joy held out her thumb and little finger and motioned back and forth. Julie knew this sign meant *Me, too.* The girls turned the corner and headed up the hill toward their neighborhood.

"Why can't they just let us do homework in detention?" Joy asked.

"I guess that's not a punishment," said Julie. "But I don't see why we couldn't do something useful, like wash chalkboards or pick up litter on the playground."

"You should be principal," said Joy, circling the letter *P* over her left hand as she said the word *principal.* Julie grinned and nodded, pleased to learn a new sign. In the few weeks since school had started, Joy had taught her quite a few signs. The signs were interesting and fun to learn, like a secret code.

At Belvedere Street, the girls went separate ways, waving good-bye. Joy signed *See you later, alligator.* Julie paused, trying to remember what Joy had shown her, then signed, *After a while, crocodile.* Joy covered her mouth, her eyes sparkling with laughter. She called, "You just said *'After a while, hippopotamus'!*"

Poster Power

In civics class the next day, Mrs. Duncan was talking about elections. "It's almost time to elect a new president," she told the class. "President Ford is hoping to stay in office for the next four years, so he's running for re-election. The candidate running against him is Jimmy Carter, who used to be governor of Georgia."

"My dad's voting for Carter," said Beth.

"My dad says he's a peanut farmer!" interrupted David. The whole class burst out laughing.

"Class," said Mrs. Duncan, "your homework assignment is to read one newspaper article about Gerald Ford and one about Jimmy Carter."

Julie raised her hand. "Are we going to vote, like in an election?"

"Yes, as a matter of fact, we are," said Mrs. Duncan. "But not for Ford or Carter," she added, flashing a rare smile. "We have school elections coming up for student body president. There will be an all-school assembly to get to know the candidates, and you'll each get to vote."

That afternoon, as Julie, Joy, and T. J. walked down the hall to their art class, Joy pointed to a new poster on the wall. It said,

You Have a STEAK in Student Government!
VOTE Salisbury for President.

"Whoa, that's Mark Salisbury," said T. J.

"Who's he?" asked Joy.

"Only the most popular kid in sixth grade and probably the whole school," T. J. replied.

Julie frowned. "Have a *steak* in government? Give me a break. It's spelled S-T-A-K-E."

T. J. rolled his eyes. "Mellow out, Albright. What are you gonna do, give out spelling demerits?"

"Well, I'm not voting for somebody who can't spell," Julie assured him.

"It's a play on words," said T. J. "*Salisbury steak*—don't you get it?"

Joy nodded. "I get it, but it's dumb."

"I agree," said Julie. "It's like the election is just a big joke to him. If I were student body president, I know the first thing *I'd* do."

"Give everyone spelling tests?" asked T. J.

"Ha, ha, very funny," said Julie. "No—I'd change the

detention system. No more writing stupid sentences a hundred times."

"Are you nuts?" asked T. J.

"I think it's a great idea," said Joy. "You should run for school president. I'd vote for you."

"Have you two lost your marbles? You have to be in *sixth* grade to be student body president," T. J. pointed out.

"Says who?" Julie asked.

"I don't know—it's just the rule," said T. J.

"For your information, girls weren't allowed on the boys' basketball team, and I got *that* rule changed," Julie pointed out.

"Well, it wouldn't matter anyway," said T. J. "You'd never beat Mark Salisbury in a million years."

"I still think you should run," said Joy. "I'll help you."

"Hey, you could be my vice president," said Julie. "We could run together. C'mon, Joy. Let's go ask the principal."

Julie clutched the red wooden hall pass as she and Joy stepped into the principal's office. Crossing the sea of gold carpet again reminded her of how scared she'd been the first time she had come to talk to Mr. Sanchez—about playing on the boys' basketball team. But when he greeted her with a smile, she instantly relaxed.

"Miss Albright," said Mr. Sanchez. "Are you getting ready for basketball season?"

Nodding her head, Julie held up the first finger on her right hand. "I hope I don't break my finger and miss the big game this year," she said.

Mr. Sanchez smiled. "I certainly hope not. And Miss Jenner, how are you liking fifth grade at Jack London?"

"So far so good," said Joy. "I'm getting a lot better at lip reading, and Julie helps me out."

"I'm glad to see you girls are friends. Now, what brings you here today?"

Julie took a deep breath. "Well, I'm thinking of running for student body president. Do you have to be in sixth grade to run?"

Mr. Sanchez raised his eyebrows. "As far as I know, there's no rule against a fifth-grader running."

"Really?" Julie said, exchanging a hopeful glance with Joy.

"It's true that the student body president has always been a sixth-grader," said the principal. "But you girls have as much right to run as anyone else."

"Can we put up posters in the hall, too?" Joy asked.

"Yes, as long as you show them to Mr. Arnold first. He's in charge of student government."

"We're on our way to art class right now—maybe we can make our first poster," said Julie.

"I think this will be a good experience for you girls,

and I wish you the best," said Mr. Sanchez, shaking their hands.

❀

Julie burst through the door of Gladrags, her mom's shop, which was right below their apartment. "Mom!" she called. "Guess what! I'm going to run for school president."

Mom finished ringing up a sale and then turned to Julie. In one breath, Julie told Mom about her exciting day. "I was wondering—can Joy come over? And is it okay to ask Ivy, too? I have to make a bunch of posters right away. The other guy already has his plastered all over the school." Ivy was Julie's best friend from her old neighborhood, where Dad lived. Julie knew Ivy would want to help.

"Posters sound like a great idea," said Mom. "There are plenty of art supplies in back. I'll be up in a little while."

"Yay, a poster party! Thanks, Mom." Julie ran upstairs to call her friends.

An hour later, Julie's living room looked like a kindergarten class. Poster boards, markers, paints, scissors, and scraps of paper littered the couch, table, and floor. The three girls sat on the rug, bent over the posters.

"Ivy, we thought up a bunch of slogans, but would you mind doing the rest of the lettering? Your printing's the best," Julie said, handing Ivy a paintbrush.

"Sure, I love doing lettering," said Ivy.

For the next half hour, the only sound in the room was the friendly squeak of markers and the snip of scissors as the three girls worked.

"How do these look?" Ivy asked, holding up a poster in each hand. *"Your future is bright with Albright,"* one poster proclaimed. *"Jump for Joy and Julie,"* said the other.

"They look great!" said Julie.

"They look like works of art!" Joy said with admiration.

"Thanks," said Ivy, flashing a smile at Joy. When the girls were finished, they stood up, brushing themselves off. They lined up the posters around the room and counted. "We have ten posters," said Ivy.

"That's twice as many as Mark has up," said Joy.

"And they look three times as good!" said Julie.

❀

On Thursday morning, Julie and Joy got to school early and proudly hung their posters in the hall, outside the library, and above the bleachers in the gym.

"What's all this?" asked T. J. as they were about to tape a poster above the fifth-grade lockers. "You can't be serious. You're really going to run for student body president against the most popular guy in the school?"

Julie and Joy exchanged a glance. "We're not afraid of that Mark guy," Joy declared.

"Besides, we have things we want to change about our school," Julie added.

"School elections aren't about changing stuff," said T. J. "They're about who's captain of the track team, or who has the most friends. It's a popularity contest. And Salisbury is *Mister* Popularity."

Julie rolled her eyes. "Are you going to stand there telling us how popular this Mark guy is, or are you going to help us put up these posters?"

"Okay, okay," said T. J. "Hand over the tape. But don't say I didn't warn you."

At lunchtime, Julie and Joy were waiting in the cafeteria line when T. J. rushed up to them. "Quick, you guys have to see this," he said urgently. The girls left their trays and ducked under the metal railing, following T. J. to the gym, where he pointed to their posters on the wall.

Julie gasped, charging up the bleachers to take a closer look. Someone had changed the name *Joy* to *Joke*. The word *vote* now read *vomit*. And there were big black mustaches on their school pictures.

"This is so mean," said Joy, slumping down onto the bleachers.

"Who would do something like this?" asked Julie, a flash of anger darkening her eyes.

"I bet I know *exactly* who did this," said T. J.

"You saw someone?" Joy asked, pointing to her eyes and signing while she spoke.

"Well, no, but at morning recess I heard Mark tell Jeff, his vice president, what a joke it is that you're running against him."

"A joke!" Julie sputtered. "What do you mean?"

"You know, because for one thing you're a fifth-grader, and for another thing, well, you're a girl." T. J. looked sheepish.

Julie glared at him. "What does being a girl have to do with it?"

"I'm just telling you what I heard," said T. J., holding up both hands defensively.

"What are we going to do now?" Joy asked. "These posters are wrecked. All that work for nothing."

"We could draw mustaches on Mark, too," T. J. suggested.

"No," said Julie. "For one thing, we don't know for sure if he's the one who did this. And besides, it's wrong."

T. J. crossed his arms and stared hard at the posters, his eyes narrowing. "Well, whoever did this should get detention, that's for sure."

"Don't say *that*," Julie groaned. "That's what I'm trying to change." She ripped a poster down from the wall.

Joy started to pull down another poster, then stopped and looked at it thoughtfully. "We might be able to save these," she said slowly.

"How?" asked T. J. "Are you two going to grow mustaches?" He flashed a silly grin.

Joy smiled. "We can just glue new pictures on that one."

"But what about this one?" Julie asked. "It says *JOKE* in really big letters."

Joy studied the poster for a moment. "How about *Voting is no JOKE.*"

"Not bad," said Julie. "I like it."

T. J. held up the poster with the word *vomit.* "I know. How about *Mark is from Planet Vomit?*"

The girls laughed. "Well, at least the other side is blank," said Julie. "Let's make a new poster right now."

"But what about lunch?" T. J. asked.

"T. J., is food all you ever think about?" Julie asked as she rolled up the poster. "C'mon, Joy, let's go."

"Wait," said T. J. "Why don't we go eat real fast and then hit the art room during recess and fix these."

"You mean you're going to help us?" asked Joy.

"And you're actually giving up *recess*?" Julie asked.

"Sure," said T. J. "We can't let Mark get away with this."

Julie smiled. She could always count on T. J.

"I can be like the guy who runs your campaign," T. J. continued. "You know, help you from behind the scenes."

"You mean like a manager?" asked Joy. "For our campaign?"

"Yep," said T. J., tearing down the last of the posters. "Campaign manager," he said slowly. "Sounds official, don't you think?"

Julie reached over and gave T. J. an exaggerated hand-shake. "I think you've got yourself a deal!"

Julie for President

 s soon as Julie got to school on Friday morning, she made a beeline for the auditorium. Mr. Arnold had suggested that she and Mark each check out the podium and test the microphone before the assembly. Backstage, Julie stood for a moment in the quiet dark. She'd have five minutes to talk about why she thought she would make a good student body president. Although she'd practiced her speech the night before, just thinking about it made her stomach do a nervous flip-flop. Closing her eyes, she imagined delivering her speech to an excited audience. Everybody hated demerits and detention, so she knew they would love her ideas. A shiver went up her spine—she could almost hear the clapping and cheering.

Just then, from behind the curtain, she heard voices. It sounded like the Water Fountain Girls—Angela, Amanda, and Alison, three girls from her class who were always hanging around the water fountain and talking about people in gossipy whispers.

"Where did he say to hang this poster?" Amanda asked, her voice bubbling with excitement.

"In the center, where the podium will be," said Angela. "There, that looks perfect. I'm voting for him for sure."

"But what about Julie?" asked Alison. "After all, she's a fifth-grader like us. Maybe we should—"

"I heard that he's going to get us a whole extra free day off from school," said Amanda.

"Sure, why not? If he can get a pool for our school, he can get a day off," Angela said confidently.

"A pool? Doesn't that cost tons of money?" asked Alison.

"Just think—we could have a swim team."

"And pool parties!" The girls squealed and giggled, jumping up and down.

"I feel kind of bad for Julie, though," said Alison. "She doesn't stand a chance."

"She might have half a chance if it weren't for that deaf girl running with her," Amanda said. "I mean, what was she thinking?"

Julie caught her breath, and her face turned hot. Just then, she heard footsteps behind her. *Joy.* Julie turned and put a finger to her lips, motioning for Joy to be quiet.

"Yeah, no one in their right mind's going to vote for

her," said Angela. "She's always waving her hands around like this." There was a pause, and the other two girls cackled. "And she sounds so weird when she talks."

"I know," Amanda agreed. "If Julie wants to get any votes at all, she better dump that deaf girl before the assembly."

Julie's face felt as if it were on fire. She hoped it was too dark backstage for Joy to see her burning cheeks.

"We'd better get to class," said Alison. "The bell's about to ring."

When Julie was sure the girls were gone, she burst through the curtain and jumped down off the stage to get a look at the poster they'd hung. Joy followed close behind. Julie couldn't look at her.

"What's wrong?" Joy asked. Her too-loud voice seemed to echo in the empty gym.

"Nothing," said Julie.

"It's those girls, isn't it?" Joy came close and touched Julie's hand. "Did they say something mean about you?"

Julie took a deep breath to calm herself. She couldn't bring herself to tell Joy they were saying mean things about *her*. But Joy read it in her face.

"Oh, I get it. They were talking about me, weren't they?" Joy asked. She was turning angry now—her hands flew in the air, signing forcefully along with each spoken word.

Clearing her throat, Julie tried to look casual. "Don't worry about them. They were just saying that we—we don't stand a chance against Mark."

"I know they don't like me," Joy said flatly. "It's because I'm deaf, isn't it?"

Julie turned to her friend, looking her straight in the eye. "I know it must be hard not being able to hear. But trust me, some things are better off not being heard."

❀

Mrs. Duncan tried to get the class to focus on Lewis and Clark, but the students were buzzing with excitement about the assembly. Julie sat silently, trying not to panic. It was almost a relief when an announcement came over the loudspeaker and Mrs. Duncan told the class to line up and walk single file to the auditorium, which was also the gym.

As the students took their seats, Mr. Arnold tapped the microphone. "Testing. Testing. Welcome, students, to the official kickoff of the 1976 election for student body president. As most of you know, this November our country will be electing a new president of the United States. And we here at Jack London Elementary are electing a new school president. Today, we'll get a chance to hear from the candidates. First up will be sixth-grader Mark Salisbury."

The audience went wild. Sixth-graders stomped their feet, rattling the bleachers and yelling, "Go, Mark! Yahoo!"

Mark stepped up to the podium and cleared his throat. "Fellow students, I know you don't want to listen to a long boring speech with lots of promises, so I promise to make this short and sweet. One word will sum up my platform." He leaned in toward the microphone. "Pizza!"

The audience clapped and cheered.

"If I'm elected president," Mark went on, "I promise to get pizza every Friday for hot lunch in the cafeteria. No more mystery meat and stewed tomatoes." Mark clapped his hands and started a chant, "Piz-za Fri-day, Piz-za Fri-day." Soon nearly all the students were clapping and chanting. Mark stepped away from the podium and took several dramatic bows, hamming it up for the audience.

Pizza? That's why he's running for school president? Julie thought to herself, but she looked out at the students and saw that they were completely swept up in the moment. Her stomach did a nervous cartwheel. All of a sudden, the speech she had prepared seemed much too serious. Maybe she should just scrap the whole thing and think up a catchy word or gimmick, as Mark had. But it was too late. Mark was already passing her on the stage with a smirk and taking his seat. Julie sat with her hands clenched in her lap, hoping to steady herself as Mr. Arnold introduced her.

"...and we thought Mark was going to run unopposed, but fifth-grader Julie Albright has decided to

make this a real contest. So let's give a warm welcome to
Julie Albright."

Several students clapped politely, but there were no
hoots or hollers as there had been for Mark. A hiss of
"fifth-grader" went through the sixth-grade bleachers.

As she stepped up to the podium, Julie reminded
herself why she was running—because of something she
believed in. Because she wanted to make her school a
better place.

"Principals, teachers, and fellow students," Julie began,
suddenly thinking of a good way to start her speech. "I
like pizza as much as anybody, but today I'm here to talk
to you about something that affects us all—detention."

"Bor-ing," a boy in the back row called out.

Swallowing hard, Julie plunged ahead. She briefly
outlined her plan to do away with detention and demerits.

The gymnasium grew dead quiet. Students looked
sideways at teachers, not sure how to react, as though they
might get in trouble for just thinking
about the idea. Then a group of
sixth-grade boys, led by Stinger,
began hooting and stomping
at the top of the bleachers.
Stinger started his own chant,
"Down with detention! Down

with detention!" but it quickly fizzled out.

Julie nervously brushed back her hair, shifting from foot to foot. "What I mean to say is, instead of sitting in detention writing sentences over and over, we could be doing something positive for our school." She looked out at the audience. Hundreds of eyes stared blankly at her.

She raised her voice a notch. "Um, we could scrub graffiti off the bathroom walls, or pick up litter—stuff like that." Still no reaction. The bright spotlight glared down on her. Julie wiped beads of sweat from her forehead. She couldn't for the life of her remember how she had been planning to end her speech. Hurriedly thanking the audience, she sat down. A few weak claps here and there seemed to mock her.

Mr. Arnold thanked her and made some final remarks. Julie didn't hear them. She fixed her eyes on the plaid pattern of his shirt and willed herself not to cry.

❀

When Julie got home from school that day, she dragged herself into the apartment, dropped her backpack, and flopped onto the couch.

"How did your speech go today, honey?" Mom asked, exchanging glances with Tracy.

"Not too good, from the looks of it," said Tracy as she headed to the kitchen for a snack.

Mom put down the laundry basket and sat on the couch next to Julie. "Tell me about it, honey."

"It was a disaster." Julie described Mark's speech about Pizza Fridays and the silent reaction to her idea. "The bad kids were the only ones who liked it!"

"You still have more than a week to go before the election," said Mom. "Anything can happen in politics. Look at Jimmy Carter. Everybody loved him after the Democratic convention this summer, and they were upset with Ford because he pardoned Nixon after Watergate."

"But I thought Nixon lied," said Julie.

"That's why a lot of people started looking at Carter. Then Carter announced that he would pardon all the Vietnam War draft dodgers—those young men who left the country rather than fight in a war they didn't believe in," Mom explained. "Now it's a much closer race."

Tracy poked her head out of the kitchen. "My civics teacher said he admires Carter for having the courage to say what he believes is right, even though it's unpopular."

"Who are you going to vote for, Mom?" Julie asked.

"I'm going to vote for Jimmy Carter," Mom told her. "I like his ideas, and I think this country needs a change."

Julie nodded. "That's what I'm trying to do for our school—make a change."

But even as she said the words, Julie knew it wouldn't

be as simple as she had thought. She remembered last year when she had tried to join the boys' basketball team. "Any time you try to change something, it's going to be difficult," her mom had warned, and she had been right.

Change had been hard to accept in her own life after her parents' divorce. It had taken time to get used to, and she'd had to find a new way of thinking about her family. Julie realized that if she wanted people to be open to her ideas, she would have to give them a new way to look at detention—a new way of thinking about it. But how?

Mom handed Julie a pile of folded laundry. "Here, honey—some clean clothes if you want to take them to Dad's this weekend. You'd better get packed. He'll be here any minute."

❀

That evening after dinner, while Julie helped Dad with the dishes, she asked, "Dad, are you going to vote for Carter or Ford for president?"

"Well, I'll tell you, I've been thinking a lot about this," said Dad. "Right now, I'm planning to vote for President Ford."

"But what about Carter?"

"Carter seems like a decent man, but we just don't know much about him," Dad answered. "And I'm not sure this country is ready for some of his new ideas. Americans have been through a lot in the past few years. I think it might be better to stick with a familiar president who knows how to run the country."

Julie dried off a dinner plate and stacked it in the cupboard. "Do you think you might change your mind?" she asked him.

"Well, so far there's been only one debate on TV, and I think Ford came out ahead on that one. But there's another debate next week, and I'll be watching it to hear what both candidates have to say."

Julie stopped drying the bowl in her hand. "How come the debates are so important?"

"In a debate, you get a much better idea of what the candidates think on all kinds of issues," Dad explained. "Tell you what—if you're interested, I'll come pick you up and we can watch the debates together."

"Really? That would be groovy," said Julie, feeling very grown-up. Tracy and her teenage friends often said *groovy*. Julie finished drying the bowl and hung up the damp towel. "And you know what, Dad? This just gave me an idea for my campaign."

Heating Up

On Monday morning, Julie and Mark had a meeting with Mr. Arnold. Julie suggested a debate between the candidates.

"I think that's a great idea, Julie," said the vice principal. But Mark looked shocked.

"You want me to debate a *girl*?" Mark said, as if Julie weren't even in the room. He put his hands on his hips. "Is there any rule that says I have to?"

"There's no rule," said Mr. Arnold. "But it would be a great opportunity for the students to get to know the candidates better."

"They already know *me*," said Mark.

"All they know is that you want pizza for school lunch," said Julie. "This would give us a chance to debate other issues we care about."

Mark wouldn't look at Julie. "Why should I help her?" he asked Mr. Arnold. "She already knows she's going to lose."

"I'm sorry you see it that way, Mark," said Mr. Arnold. "I think a debate would be a terrific experience. I'd like you to think it over."

"Sorry," said Mark, turning to go. "Not interested."

❀

As Julie headed down the hall toward her locker, she felt disappointment dragging her steps.

"You look like we just lost a basketball game or something," said T. J. He and Joy were standing near Julie's locker, waiting for her. As they walked to class, Julie started to tell her friends about the debate.

"Whoa," said T. J., his face lighting up. "That's a great idea."

"You're brave," said Joy. "It would be hard to get up in front of all those people again and debate Mark."

"Doesn't matter," Julie sighed. "Mark said no."

T. J. stopped in his tracks. "What do you mean he said no?"

Julie shrugged. "He knows he's going to win, so why should he debate me?"

"If he's so sure, then why's he afraid to debate you?" T. J. asked.

"He doesn't want to, and he doesn't have to," said Julie.

"We just have to think up another way to get our ideas across," said Joy.

"Like this," said T. J. He reached into his backpack and pulled out two buttons that said *NO DETENTION*.

"You made these?" asked Joy. "For us?"

"My dad has a button-making machine," said T. J. "I was thinking you guys could wear these. You'll be like walking ads. Maybe it'll help get your ideas out."

"Wow," said Julie, pinning her button to her sweater. "Thanks, T. J."

"Hey, what are campaign managers for?" T. J. bobbed his head, a hunk of sandy hair flopping over his eyes, and smiled ear to ear.

"I have an idea," said Joy. "Maybe we could stand by the front door after school and talk to kids as they get on their buses. We can wear our buttons and tell them about changing the detention system."

"Brilliant," Julie said, grinning.

❖

When the school day was over and the final bell rang, Julie and Joy headed to the front lobby. Kids started pouring down the halls and out the front door.

"No more detention," Julie called out as kids filed past her. "Vote for Julie. Change the system."

Kids hurried past her, eager to get to their buses. *Nobody's even listening*, thought Julie. She peeled one of their posters off the wall and turned to Joy. "Here, hold this poster out so all the kids will see it, while I do the talking."

Julie went up to a group of kids and asked them what they thought about demerits and detention. The students stared silently at her. Nervously, she glanced at Joy, who stood stiffly, barely holding up the poster.

A boy in a red jacket bumped into Joy and gave her an unfriendly look. "Hey, watch out. You're blocking the way."

"Joy," said Julie impatiently, "Can't you hold up the poster like I said?"

Joy let the poster drop. As she spoke, her hands flew so fast that Julie had to step back to get out of the way. *I may be deaf, but I can still speak for myself.*

"Sorry," said Julie. "I didn't mean—never mind. Don't worry about the poster. Let's both talk to as many kids as we can. There's not much time before the buses leave."

Joy stood by the other set of doors. "Hi, I'm Joy Jenner," she started, but Julie watched the kids brush right past her. "Vote for Julie for school president," Joy tried again. The kids began heading out the opposite door to avoid walking past her.

"Who is that girl, anyway?" asked a girl in a corduroy jumper.

"When she talks, she sounds like she's inside a fish-bowl," said another.

"Maybe her name's Flipper!" said a boy, and he began singing the *Flipper* theme song all the way to the bus. "*They call her Flipper, Flipper, faster than lightning . . .*"

Julie crumpled inside. She had known that the other

kids thought Joy was weird, strange, different. What she hadn't realized—until now, seeing it with her own eyes—was that this made them a little bit afraid of her.

Watching the kids skirt around Joy to the other exit, Julie suddenly felt dizzy with uncertainty. She knew it wouldn't be right to ask Joy not to speak up for herself. But Julie had to admit that when Joy did speak, it made things worse. The truth was, having Joy for a vice president was ruining any chance she had at being elected student body president—or even at getting kids to think about her ideas. But how on earth could she tell her friend that?

❁

As soon as she got home, Julie dropped her backpack inside the front door and went straight to her room, fighting back tears. A few minutes later, she heard Tracy yell, "Hey, why'd you dump your stuff in the middle of the doorway? I almost tripped and broke my—" But when Tracy got to Julie's room and saw her sister's face, she stopped.

"Jules?" she asked softly. "Are you okay?"

Julie didn't answer. Tracy sat down on the bed next to her. "Did something happen at school? Do you want to talk about it?"

"It's the election," Julie said dully. "Nobody gets my ideas, and Mark, the guy I'm running against, won't even be in a debate with me. Then today, when Joy and I tried to talk to kids about our ideas, everybody acted like we had major cooties."

"Cooties?" Tracy asked, trying to hold back a little smile.

"It's not funny!" said Julie. "It's like they think Joy has a disease and they're afraid they'll catch it. They look at her like she's weird. They call her names and say awful stuff about her, and she can't even hear them."

"I know—kids can be so mean," said Tracy. "In high school, some people are mean if they think you wear the wrong clothes." She reached over and smoothed out the bedspread between them.

"It's all a huge mess," Julie moaned. "I hate to say it, but I even started thinking maybe I should ask T. J. to run with me instead. I don't have a chance of winning with Joy as my vice president. Of course, I probably wouldn't win anyway. And I don't want to lose her as a friend." With a groan, Julie fell back on her bed. "Why did I ever think running for student body president was a good idea? It's the worst idea I've ever had."

❁

The next morning, when Julie and Joy passed through the front doors of the school, they stopped, stunned.

Mark and Jeff stood at the front door, shaking hands with kids as they poured off the buses and headed for their

"It's the election," Julie said dully. *"Nobody gets my ideas."*

classrooms. "I'm Mark Salisbury, your next student body president," Mark said, smiling with a big, toothy grin.

"He stole our idea!" said Joy.

Julie nodded but didn't say a word.

At their lockers, Julie turned to Joy. "We might as well admit it—Mark has us beat. He's going to win by a land-slide. Let's just drop out of the race now and not give that Pizza Monster the satisfaction of eating us alive." Julie forced herself to meet Joy's eyes.

Joy looked surprised. She searched Julie's face. "That's not like you to quit," Joy said finally.

"I know, but—well, nothing has turned out the way I expected. It just seems like dropping out is the best thing to do now." *Please don't make this harder than it already is,* Julie begged silently.

"It's me, isn't it?" Joy looked at the floor. "I may be deaf, but I'm not blind. Nobody likes me. I'm the one they avoid. They don't even give you a chance because of me."

Julie buried her head in her locker so that Joy wouldn't see the truth of it on her face.

"If anybody drops out, it should be me," Joy went on. "You can ask T. J. to be your vice president. He's on the basketball team with you, and everybody likes him. But most of all, he's not deaf."

Julie wanted to protest, but instead she heard herself

mumble, "Um, the bell's about to ring. We'd better get to class."

❀

In social studies, Julie willed herself to focus on Lewis and Clark's journey. She had to admit it *was* pretty exciting. They had faced wild bears and raging rivers and months of hardship. It reminded Julie of her wagon train trip last summer for the Bicentennial, although she knew that Lewis and Clark's expedition had been far more dangerous than hers.

"'Courage undaunted, possessing a firmness and perseverance of purpose,'" said Mrs. Duncan. "That's how Thomas Jefferson, who was president, described Meriwether Lewis. What did he mean by that?"

The students squirmed in their seats, looking blankly at the teacher. Slowly, one hand rose.

"Joy?" said Mrs. Duncan.

"I think he meant that Lewis was brave," Joy said slowly in her odd voice, "and that he didn't give up." She glanced sideways at Julie.

Julie blinked in surprise. Joy almost never spoke up in class. Was her friend trying to send her a message?

❀

At lunch, T. J. raced up to Julie and Joy. "You're not going to believe this," he said, cutting in line next to them.

"Did you see the signs I put up this morning that say 'Where's the Debate?' Everybody's buzzing about it—and now they want a debate."

"Are you serious?" Julie asked.

T. J. nodded. "Get this—Jeff, Mark's own vice president, asked him why he's afraid to debate a girl. And guess what? Mark didn't know what to say, so he finally agreed to do it. You got your debate!"

"Too bad somebody's dropping out of the election," said Joy.

"What? Who—you?" T. J. asked, looking from Joy to Julie.

"I didn't say it was for sure," said Julie defensively. She couldn't admit that she'd been thinking about letting Joy drop out.

"You can't quit now," said T. J. "The election's just heating up!"

T. J. and Joy were right, thought Julie. She couldn't quit now.

❀

"D-day," T. J. said, coming up to Julie in the hall on Thursday morning.

"Huh?" Julie turned and gave him a blank look.

"Debate Day." He elbowed her in the ribs with a good-natured grin.

Julie bit her bottom lip. Now that the debate was here, her stomach fluttered with nervous anticipation. But she reminded herself that this was the best way to get her ideas across, and that steadied her.

When it was time for the debate, Julie took her place onstage at a podium with Mark. She squinted in the bright spotlight, looking out over the rows of students until she spotted Joy and T. J. in the audience. T. J. had told her it might help to fix her eyes on a friendly face or two at first.

Mr. Arnold gave a short introduction, explaining the ground rules and time limits of the debate. He would ask a question, and each candidate would have a turn to answer. "Please hold your applause until the very end," said Mr. Arnold. "Now, first question: Why is student government important? Miss Albright, we'll begin with you."

Leaning in to the microphone, Julie said, "Student government is important because it gives all of us a say in what happens at our school."

"Mr. Salisbury?"

"Student government is important because we get to plan fun activities, like going to Marine World."

The crowd clapped and cheered, and Mr. Arnold had to remind them to hold their applause.

"Julie," said Mr. Arnold, glancing at his index cards,

"Pizza's great!" said Julie. "I just think there are more important things to do, like changing the detention system."

"Mark has proposed Pizza Fridays as his platform. Tell us what you think of his idea."

"Pizza's great!" said Julie. "I just think there are more important things to do, like changing the detention system."

"Thank you, Julie. Mr. Salisbury, your comments on Julie's idea to change the detention system?"

"She doesn't know what she's talking about," said Mark.

"Yes, I do," said Julie. "I've *been* to detention." The crowd laughed. "That's how I know we need to change it."

"Julie, I'm going to have to ask you to wait your turn to speak," Mr. Arnold cautioned.

"Sorry," said Julie, blushing.

"If we didn't have detention," said Mark, "then all the bullies could do whatever they wanted, and the bad kids would take over the school. Everybody knows that. Or at least by the time you get to sixth grade, you do." He turned to face the audience. "Think about it—do you really want a student body president and vice president who have both been in detention?"

"Mr. Arnold," said Julie, raising her hand. "May I say one more thing?"

Mr. Arnold looked at his watch. "I'll allow a rebuttal. You have one minute."

Julie took a deep breath. The audience was silent, watching. And listening. "Of course if a student does something wrong, there has to be a consequence," she began. "But I don't see how sitting in detention and writing the same sentence a hundred times helps anybody. What I am saying is that if we break a rule, we should make up for it by doing something good, instead of something useless that just gives you writer's cramp."

"Your one minute is up," said Mr. Arnold. "Mark, you have one minute to reply."

"Detention isn't supposed to be fun," said Mark. "It's supposed to be a punishment."

"But we should learn from our mistakes," said Julie. "And I think we'd learn more if we did something useful. Something that helps the whole school."

To Julie's surprise, the students burst into applause. Mr. Arnold had to quiet them down once more.

"Okay, let's move on," said Mr. Arnold. "Final question: If for some reason you had to leave the office of student body president, your vice president would take your place. Please tell us what qualifies him or her for this position. Mark?"

"Easy," said Mark. "My VP, Jeff Coopersmith, is captain of the crossing guards. Everybody knows him, and he's real tall so it would be easy to find him when you need him." Everyone laughed.

"Thank you, Mark. Julie, can you tell us what qualifies

your vice president to be student body president?"

Julie froze. The whole audience seemed to hold its breath. For one long, awkward moment, all eyes were on Julie, waiting. In the vast quiet, Julie began to talk. "My vice president, Joy Jenner, is new to our school. Because she's new, many of you haven't gotten to know her. Instead of speaking for her, I'd like to ask her to come up to the podium and speak for herself."

In utter silence, all heads turned to watch Joy as she walked down the center aisle between the rows of folding chairs and up onto the stage. Julie stepped back from the microphone. Joy gripped the podium, as if steadying herself in a strong wind. She took a deep breath. When she opened her mouth, nothing came out.

Julie reached over and gave Joy's hand a soft squeeze. The whole audience seemed to sit closer, leaning in to hear Joy's words.

"I know I'm different," Joy started. "I know I talk funny. I can't hear what you hear because I'm deaf. But everybody feels different sometimes. And even though I'm deaf, I promise to listen to you. I hope you'll give me a chance."

Wow! Great job, Julie signed to Joy as Mr. Arnold thanked everyone and wrapped up the assembly.

As Julie's class headed down the hall to their classroom, Mrs. Duncan lingered to congratulate the girls. "Julie, you did us proud in Room 5D." Julie beamed at the rare praise from her teacher. Then Mrs. Duncan turned to Joy. "Joy, I know it was difficult for you to speak in front of the whole school, but you really shined."

"Thanks," said Joy. She touched a hand to her chin, signing *thank you* with a shy smile.

As they approached their classroom, Julie heard a commotion inside. Through the open door, she could see the Water Fountain Girls standing in front of the whole class. Alison was holding out a bottle of glue like a microphone, and Amanda was speaking into it using a loud, nasal voice to imitate Joy at the podium during the debate. Angela was flailing her arms about in mock sign language.

"What in the world!" Mrs. Duncan barked. The three girls turned, red-faced. Marching into the classroom, Mrs. Duncan blinked the lights on and off and clapped sharply to get the class settled down. "Class! That is e-nough," she said, each syllable as sharp as her clapping. "At this school, we respect others, despite our differences."

In horror, Julie glanced at Joy. Joy's face twisted with pain, and she rushed off down the hall. "Joy, wait up," Julie called, hurrying after her. But her words just echoed down the empty corridor, unheard.

Julie found Joy crumpled on the floor in a corner of the girls' bathroom. She knelt beside her on the cold tile and gently put a hand on Joy's shoulder.

Finally, Joy raised her tear-stained face. "I did my best, but it wasn't enough. They think I'm stupid—stupid like a clown." She put her head in her arms and sobbed.

Julie swallowed, her eyes welling with sympathy. She didn't know what she could say to help Joy feel better. Finally, she said, "Last year, when I was the new girl, those same girls said mean stuff about me, too. I know how you  feel." But even as Julie spoke the words, she wasn't so sure. It was one thing to have the Water Fountain Girls talk about you behind your back in the halls or at the water fountain. It was another thing for them to make fun of someone in front of the whole class.

Joy looked away. "I can't go back there, ever."

"Joy, listen—you can't hide in the girls' bathroom forever. Pretty soon the lunch bell will ring and there'll be a ton of kids in here."

Joy pulled herself up. "I don't feel so good," she said, clutching her stomach.

Julie put her arm around Joy. "Come on, I'll walk you to the nurse's office."

When Julie got back to class, Mrs. Duncan stepped out into the hall with her. "Where's Joy? Is she all right?"

Julie shook her head. "She has a stomach ache, so she's lying down in the nurse's office."

Mrs. Duncan rubbed her forehead. "I'll check on her later. Let's give her some time to herself. It was terribly hurtful what those girls did. They will have to apologize to Joy."

Julie nodded and headed to her seat. She flushed as she felt eyes on her, and she stared straight ahead to avoid making eye contact with the Water Fountain Girls. She tried to concentrate on her math worksheet, but none of the columns seemed to add up.

❁

Julie stared at the sloppy joe on her lunch tray. She hadn't touched a bite of her food.

T. J. plopped his tray down next to Julie's. "Boy oh boy, I've never seen Duncan Donut so mad. When you and Joy were gone, she really blasted those girls. You should have seen it. She was practically spitting when she gave them detention."

Julie looked up from her tray. "They got detention?"

"More like triple detention. They have to write 'I will

not make fun of others' three hundred times. That's like six pages front and back!"

"Oh, no." Julie put her head in her hands.

"What!? They deserve it!" T. J. said heatedly. "You guys were boss in that debate. You beat the pants off Mark, and all they did was make fun of you." He took a big bite of his sloppy joe.

"That's not the point, T. J.," Julie moaned.

"Listen, Julie," T. J. said with his mouth full. "I know you're against detention, but this time they really deserve it."

Julie hated to admit it, but part of her did want to see the Water Fountain Girls punished.

T. J. leaned across the table toward her. "Are you saying they should get away with it?"

Julie shook her head. It was starting to ache. She took a sip of her chocolate milk.

"Well?" T. J. asked, still waiting for an answer.

"T. J., if those girls do a dumb detention where they write the same sentence a million times, how will that help anything? Will it make them sorry for what they did? You know it won't—it'll just make them hate Joy more than ever. After all, if it wasn't for her, they wouldn't be stuck in detention in the first place. That's how they'll see it."

"I guess," T. J. shrugged. "That's just how kids are."

"And that's why detention doesn't work."

"Well, okay then, Miss Smartypants," said T. J. "If you were Mrs. Duncan, what would *you* do?"

Julie rubbed her forehead. "I'm not sure."

"Good thing it's not up to you, then," said T. J. "Hey, can I have your sloppy joe if you're not going to eat it?"

Julie pushed her plate toward T. J. "Here." She got up. "I'm going to see how Joy's doing."

But when she got to the nurse's office, the cot was empty, and the nurse told Julie that Joy had gone home.

The Election

❀ **Chapter 10** ❀

That afternoon, Julie was grateful that her class made a trip to the library. Even though she missed giggling in the corner with Joy, it gave her some quiet time to think. And her thoughts were in a tangle. As much as she wanted to see the Water Fountain Girls pay for what they'd done, she knew in her heart that detention wasn't the answer. Writing sentences wouldn't change the Water Fountain Girls at all, or make school better for Joy.

But what *was* the answer? Over and over in her head she heard T. J.'s words—*If you were Mrs. Duncan, what would you do?*

Julie looked around the library, groping for an idea. She scanned the books on the back wall. Biographies. *Anne Frank: The Diary of a Young Girl. And Then What Happened, Paul Revere?* She stared at the shelves in front of her. Languages. *How to Speak Spanish.*

Languages. It was as if Joy spoke a foreign language— one that the Water Fountain Girls did not understand.

But what if they could speak her language? Maybe if they got to know Joy, they wouldn't act so cruel.

❀ *103* ❀

"Last call for checking out books," called Mrs. Paterson, the librarian, startling Julie out of her deep thought.

Julie hopped up. She did want to check out a book, if she could find the right one. Running her fingers along the spines, she saw it: *Sign Language Is Fun*. She took it to the checkout desk. Suddenly, she knew how to answer T. J.'s question. Now she just had to get Mrs. Duncan to go along with her idea.

❀

The final bell rang. While the other students gathered their books and clunked their chairs upside down on their desks, the Water Fountain Girls trudged off to detention.

"Mrs. Duncan?" Julie asked, hugging her books to her chest as she approached the teacher's desk. "May I ask you a question?"

"What is it, Julie?" Her teacher sounded tired.

"Mrs. Duncan," Julie repeated, "I know what those girls did was wrong, and they hurt Joy a lot. But I've been thinking—um, well, how is writing sentences going to help them learn from what they did or make them act better in the future?"

"I'm not sure what you're suggesting, Julie. I know you have a low opinion of detention, but it will force those girls to write and think about what they've done."

"Will it?" asked Julie. "Just look at Stinger—detention

doesn't seem to be making *him* act any better. Last year, you gave him forty-three detentions, and he hasn't changed one bit."

"Well, I'll give you that," said Mrs. Duncan, gathering up the folders on her desk and sliding them into her tote bag. "All right, Julie. Go ahead—tell me what you're thinking."

Julie held up her library book for Mrs. Duncan to see. "I was thinking I could teach them some sign language."

Mrs. Duncan's eyes widened with surprise, but Julie kept right on talking. "Joy taught me lots of signs, and I'm learning even more from this book. Maybe if the girls learned some sign language, it would help them understand Joy a little better, and they wouldn't feel like she's so weird or different anymore . . ." Julie stopped twisting the hem of her shirt and looked anxiously at Mrs. Duncan. Was her teacher angry with her?

Mrs. Duncan was quiet. She picked up her grade book and put it in her bag. Julie felt certain that the creases in her teacher's forehead were disapproving. Finally, Mrs. Duncan set down her tote bag. She looked up at Julie and said, "You know what? Maybe this is worth a try." She scribbled out a note and handed it to Julie. "Go to the library and give this note to Mr. Arnold. Ask the girls to come back to the classroom. I can stay an extra hour today."

"Really? You mean it?" Julie let out a breath. "Thank you, Mrs. Duncan."

"No, thank you," said Mrs. Duncan. "After twenty-three years of teaching, I just might be learning something new."

❖

The Water Fountain Girls were leery as they followed Julie back to the classroom.

"What did you pull us out of detention for?" Angela huffed.

"We weren't even half done writing our sentences. You better not be getting us in more trouble," said Amanda.

"You want to go back there?" Julie snapped. "Go right ahead—be my guest. Excuse me for thinking maybe you'd rather do something besides write a million sentences till your hands fall off. Not that you don't deserve it."

"What do you mean?" Alison asked.

"Are you saying you're going to get us out of writing all those sentences?" asked Angela. "Why would you be nice to us? What's the catch?"

Julie glared at her. "All you think about are yourselves. Did you ever stop to think for one minute about Joy—that I might be doing something for *her*, not for you?"

As Julie explained her idea, Angela rolled her eyes and Amanda stood with her hand on her hip. Alison just stared at the floor. When Julie was finished, there was a long, uncomfortable silence.

Finally Alison looked up at her friends. "Well, at least this sounds better than detention."

"I guess," said Amanda reluctantly.

"It's not like we really have a choice," Angela muttered as they followed Julie into Mrs. Duncan's room.

Alison, Amanda, and Angela pulled their chairs to form a semicircle around Julie. She started out by helping each girl create a unique sign for her name. Then she showed them a few simple signs, like *hello* and *please*. Next, Julie looked up signs in her library book for objects around the room—clock, window, desk, hamster—and showed them how to make the hand signs.

"This is hard," Angela grumbled. "I can't make my fingers work right."

"I'll teach you how to finger-spell," Julie said. Soon she, Alison, Amanda, and Angela were singing "*A-B-C-D-E-F-G,*" moving their hands in time to the song and trying to remember the finger positions for each letter. They ran through the song a few times, faster and faster, and ended breathless and laughing.

"I never in a million years thought I'd be singing the alphabet song in fifth grade!" Alison exclaimed.

"My fingers are all tangled up," Amanda giggled.

Even Angela cracked a small smile.

"Girls, I'm afraid that's all the time we have for today," said Mrs. Duncan.

The four girls were quiet as they put their chairs back up onto the desks and gathered their belongings.

Alison leaned on the rungs of her upside-down chair for a moment and breathed a heavy sigh. "Julie?" she started softly. "Does this mean you're not mad at us?"

Julie hesitated for a moment. Then she rubbed her thumb against her index finger.

"What does that mean?" Alison asked.

"A little bit," Julie said.

Alison looked grateful and gave Julie a quick smile.

Amanda had edged closer. Suddenly she blurted out, "Do you think Joy will ever forgive us for what we did?"

"I don't know," Julie answered.

Alison spoke up again. "Before we go, will you show us how to sign the word *sorry*?"

"Okay, sure," said Julie. "First, make the letter *A*." She held out a fist with her thumb facing up. "Then rub it in a circle over your heart."

All three girls watched Julie intently. Then, carefully, they formed their hands into the letter *A* and made circles over their hearts.

❁

On Friday morning, when Julie arrived at school, Amanda, Alison, and Angela were waiting in the lobby. They rushed up to her.

"Where's Joy?" Angela demanded.

"She's coming today, right?" asked Amanda.

Julie shook her head. "I stopped by her house on the way to school, but her mother said she still isn't feeling well."

"But it's Friday—that means we won't see her until Monday," said Alison, looking distressed. The three girls exchanged a glance.

"We can't wait till Monday," said Angela. "We have to tell her we're sorry."

"We *want* to tell her," Alison added.

Julie shifted her backpack, thinking.

"Hey, Julie," said Amanda, "do you think we could have detention again today?"

"Huh?" Julie asked. "You mean—"

"Yeah, you know, stay after school, like yesterday, and learn more signs," Amanda explained.

Julie looked up, startled, and then broke into a grin. "Oh, so you think my idea for changing detention is better than Pizza Fridays?"

The three girls looked sheepish at first. Then Angela

said, "Well, duh!" and all four girls laughed.

"Tell you what," said Julie. "Why don't we hold detention at Joy's house after school today. Maybe we can cheer
her up."

After school, the four girls walked to Joy's house. Julie
rang the bell, which made a light flash inside the house
for Joy to see. Amanda hung back, and Alison and Angela
shuffled nervously behind Julie.

Joy opened the door. "Julie! Come on in. What are
you—" Then her face went white as she saw the other girls.
She stood stiffly, with the door half open.

"It's okay," said Julie, reaching for Joy's hand. Joy pulled
back as if she'd been burned.

"Joy, please let us in," said Angela, stepping forward.
"We just want to talk to you."

"We came to say we're sorry," said Alison, rubbing her
heart with her fist. Angela and Amanda quickly joined in.

Joy's dark eyes welled up as she opened the door wider.

Sitting on the floor around the coffee table in the front
room, the Water Fountain Girls told Joy how sorry they
were. Julie could see in their faces that they meant it, and
she knew Joy could see it, too.

Joy's mother came in with mugs of hot chocolate, and
soon the room was filled with chatter and signing.

"What I don't get is how did the three of you learn all

this sign language?" asked Joy, her forehead crinkling.

Julie told Joy about the new detention.

"And it really worked!" said Alison and Angela at the same time. All the girls laughed.

When it was time to go, the girls took their mugs to the kitchen and thanked Mrs. Jenner. On their way out the door, Alison turned to Julie. "What's the sign for *friend*?"

Julie showed her how to hook index fingers to say *friend* in sign language. Alison reached over and hooked her finger with Joy's. As they locked fingers, a fleeting trace of a smile passed over Joy's face, like sun peeking through a cloud.

❖

On Monday morning, Julie and Joy walked to school together. Even though it was election day and Julie was anxious, at least Joy was back at school. No matter what happened, they'd face it together.

As they entered the school building, Julie saw T. J. at the edge of a crowd of students. He waved, but instead of coming over, he turned and called, "They're here!"

The crowd parted, and there in the middle of the lobby stood the Water Fountain Girls, dressed from head to toe in green and blue, the school colors.

"From the top. One, two, three!" called Angela as she,

Amanda, and Alison led the crowd in a song:

> *If you're happy and you know it, vote for Julie.*
> *If you're happy and you know it, jump for Joy.*
> *If you're happy and you know it,*
> *Then your VOTE will really show it.*
> *If you're happy and you know it . . .*
> *VOTE FOR JULIE! JUMP FOR JOY!*

Everybody clapped and cheered.

Joy touched the tips of both hands to her mouth and extended them out in gratitude, signing *thank you* to the three girls.

"Wow, thanks, you guys!" said Julie. "That was really neat."

"Yeah, I wish I'd thought of it," said T. J., "but they came up with it on their own. Isn't it great? Now lots of people are saying they're going to vote for you guys."

Julie looked around. Students were humming the catchy tune as they drifted off to their lockers and classes. Her opponent, Mark, was nowhere to be seen.

❁

It took all day for each classroom to vote and for Mr. Arnold to tally the results. More than once, Julie caught herself staring at the loudspeaker on the wall, willing it to call everyone to the assembly so Mr. Arnold could announce the winner. At last, the familiar crackle came over the PA system, and Julie heard the vice principal's voice.

"Students, we have the results of the election that you've all been waiting to hear. Starting with grade one, please make your way down to the auditorium as quietly as possible."

As soon as they were seated at the assembly, Julie asked Joy, "What's the sign for *butterflies*?" Joy crossed her hands, linking her thumbs and wiggling her fingers. Julie made the sign for *butterflies* and then pointed to her stomach to show Joy how nervous and excited she felt. Joy gave her a thumbs-up, wishing her good luck.

Mr. Arnold stepped up to the podium. "In all my years as head of student government, this has been one of the most exciting school elections at Jack London Elementary. All the candidates did an outstanding job and certainly gave us a lot to think about. There can only be one winner today, but everyone who participated in the election is a winner."

A first-grader in the front row blurted out, "Who won? The boy or the girl?" The students burst out in laughter.

Mr. Arnold smiled. "To answer that question—" he paused for dramatic effect and then went on, "I would like to extend my sincere congratulations to the 1976

Jack London Elementary student body president and vice president, Miss Julie Albright and Miss Joy Jenner! Please join me on the stage." The audience erupted with applause.

Julie and Joy hugged each other and then ran up the steps onto the stage to shake hands with Mr. Arnold. When the applause died down, the students of Room 5D suddenly rose to their feet, a small oasis in the center of the audience. Their hands, like fluttering leaves, waved in silent celebration as they applauded in sign language.

Looking out over the sea of teachers, classmates, and friends, Julie thought about all the changes the past year had held for her—a new school, a new home, and hardest of all, a new way of being a family. She smiled wistfully, remembering how hard it had been, at first, to stop wishing things would somehow go back to the way they used to be. But over the past year, she had learned that she didn't have to be afraid of change.

Change was different, and it was hard—sometimes sad, even painful—but it was also an invitation to think new thoughts, to see things in a new way, to grow. Even to become a better person. And all the changes had brought her to this moment. She was now the student body president!

Suddenly, T. J. dashed up onto the stage and yanked on a dangling rope. Bright balloons and confetti fluttered down, swirling around her.

"T. J., how on earth did you pull that off?" Julie asked him, laughing.

"Oh, Mr. Arnold and I had it all planned, no matter who won. But I had my fingers crossed that it would be you." He batted at a balloon and gave her a cocky grin. "This is how they do it for real when the president gets elected. One day that's going to be me—campaign manager for the president of the United States."

"You're hired!" said Julie. "When I run for president someday, there's nobody I'd rather have running my campaign."

The wagon train that Julie and April rode in was a real event. The idea behind it was to inspire Americans to think about their country's history by traveling across the country the same way the pioneers did—by wagon train! Only this time the wagons would travel from west to east, to "bring the country back to its birthplace." The Pennsylvania Bicentennial Commission delivered an official state wagon to all 50 states, and the wagons toured around each state, passing out the rededication scrolls. In Hawaii, people took scrolls to the outer islands by outrigger canoe, and in Alaska, the scrolls were carried by dogsled!

In the summer of 1975, the first wagons began heading

east. Private wagons and riders traveled with the official state wagons, just as April's family did in the story. Along the way, local people helped provide meals, shelter, and water for the horses. By spring 1976, the wagon trains began joining together in the middle of the country. Julie's story is set during the last segment of the long journey, from Pittsburgh to Valley Forge.

On July 4, 1976, cities and towns across America celebrated the Bicentennial with picnics, parties, and parades. In Sheboygan, Wisconsin, children watched as 1,776 Frisbees went whizzing off a hill. Baltimore served up a 75,000-pound, 90-foot-long birthday cake in the shape of the United States. At 2:00 p.m. eastern time, bells rang all around the country to commemorate the moment when the Liberty Bell had sounded the nation's independence 200 years earlier. And families everywhere watched on TV as fireworks exploded over Washington, D.C.

Some people saw the Bicentennial as a business opportunity, much like Mr. Higgins in the story. In addition to Bicentennial souvenirs, thousands of ordinary products came with patriotic themes. You could buy a teddy bear that recited the Pledge of Allegiance, and even a "Spirit of '76" coffin in red, white, and blue!

Some Americans felt that it was wrong to cash in on the country's birthday, which they started calling the "buy-centennial." Others questioned whether the nation's founding was something to celebrate. Some Native American communities chose to commemorate their history instead. Many people wondered whether Americans, so deeply divided by the Vietnam War and the Watergate scandal, could unite in celebration. The summer of 1976 proved they could: that Americans loved their country despite its problems and felt connected to their fellow citizens despite their differences.

In his speech at Valley Forge, President Gerald Ford called this shared experience "our American adventure." He hailed the pioneer

President Ford at Valley Forge

settlers and the patriots at Valley Forge for their "spirit of sacrifice and self-discipline." After her own adventure on the wagon train, Julie would have known just what he meant!

Many African Americans voted for Carter, who had been a popular governor in Georgia. (The sign's backward R's are a play on the logo of Toys"R"Us, a popular store in the 1970s.)

That fall, President Ford ran for relection against former Georgia governor Jimmy Carter. Children like Julie watched the candidates campaign and debate their ideas about how the country should be run. Ford had more political experience than Carter, but he had been Nixon's vice president, so Ford was closely linked to President Nixon's failings. Many voters felt Carter represented a new direction for the country.

When Jimmy Carter was elected president, the nation faced some serious challenges. High *inflation*—an increase in the price of goods and services—made it harder for people to afford the things they needed. At the same time, millions of American workers lost their jobs as U.S. companies moved overseas, where workers could be hired for less. Increased competition from foreign companies, especially in cars and electronics, hurt American companies and workers. And a worldwide oil shortage led to high heating costs and gas prices. Carter encouraged Americans to

Service stations had to ration, or restrict, gas sales.

Shirley Chisholm

start using other energy sources such as coal, wind, solar, or nuclear power, and to *conserve*, or save, energy. These issues are still part of our lives today.

Along with a new president, there were other new faces in government as women and minorities began running—and getting elected. Congresswoman Shirley Chisholm ran in the 1972 presidential election. Although she didn't win, she showed that women, including women of color, could be seriously considered as candidates.

The decade also brought positive changes for people with disabilities. For years, people with disabilities could not go to regular schools or get jobs, making it hard for them to live independent lives. Children who were blind or deaf like Joy or who had other disabilities usually didn't attend the same schools or classes as other children.

In 2007, California Congresswoman Nancy Pelosi became the first woman Speaker of the House of Representatives. Her grandchildren watched her get sworn in.

As girls in the 1970s, actress Marlee Matlin, left, and 1995 Miss America Heather Whitestone, right, were teased for being deaf. They didn't let it stop them! Heather is signing "I love you."

One girl, Judy Heumann, knew that her classmates viewed her as "the girl in the wheelchair" and felt awkward around her. In 1970, at age 22, Judy started a group called Disabled in Action to raise awareness and fight for the rights of people with disabilities. She wanted to change attitudes and show that having a disability didn't mean you couldn't lead a productive life. Thanks to activists like Judy, new laws were passed to give people with disabilities greater access to the world around them.

The desire to make the world a better place is still alive today. Like Julie Albright, children and grown-ups work hard to improve their schools, serve in the government, and help others in need. While the country still faces many of the problems it did in Julie's time, Americans of all ages, races, abilities, and political viewpoints continue to tackle these issues with optimism and creativity. They don't always agree with one another, but they usually share the same basic goal—to make their country truly a place of justice, freedom, and equality.

a Nez Perce girl who loves daring adventures on horseback

a Jewish girl with a secret ambition to be an actress

who joins the war effort when Hawaii is attacked

whose big ideas get her into trouble—but also save the day

who finds the strength to lift her voice for those who can't

who fights for the right to play on the boys' basketball team